I'LL ALWAYS BE THERE

When Becca is persuaded to attend a speed-dating evening, she has no notion of the chain of events it will set in motion. She meets three men: Marco, Gary and Andy. Marco introduces her to wealthy entrepreneur Lando Wheatley, who turns out to be the landlord of the beauty salon she runs with her friend Lizzie. Then there's Sam, Lizzie's brother, who she once dated. When someone begins to stalk her, Becca doesn't know which of the men she can trust, and which might have an out-of-control possessive streak . . .

SUSAN UDY

I'LL ALWAYS BE THERE

Complete and Unabridged

LINFORD
Leicester

First published in Great Britain in 2018

First Linford Edition
published 2018

A catalogue record for this book is available
from the British Library.

ISBN 978–1–4448–3719–3

Published by
F. A. Thorpe (Publishing)
Anstey, Leicestershire

Set by Words & Graphics Ltd.
Anstey, Leicestershire
Printed and bound in Great Britain by
T. J. International Ltd., Padstow, Cornwall

This book is printed on acid-free paper

1

'I know you're seeing other men,' the voice hissed into Becca's ear, 'so I'm warning you. I'll always be there, somewhere nearby, watching, waiting. You're mine, and sooner or later you'll have to admit that and stop wasting both our lives. We can be together. We should be together. Why can't you see that?'

Horrified, and more than a little scared, Becca Seymour slammed the receiver back onto its base, cutting the phone call short. However, she couldn't stop her thoughts rushing back to one evening two and a half weeks ago. An evening that she had a sneaking suspicion could have given rise to this almost threatening phone call.

Of course, the whole thing had been Lizzie's idea. Becca would never have attended such an event on her own.

'Come on,' Lizzie had urged. 'Let's give it a go. It'll be fun. And who knows who we'll meet. Jenny Richmond went to one and met Rick. Look at them now. Engaged to be married and all within two months.'

'Exactly,' Becca snapped. 'Too quick by half. She must barely know him.'

'Don't be such a stick in the mud. There is such a thing as love at first sight.'

'Firstly, I'm not a stick in the mud, and secondly, I don't believe in love at first sight. In my opinion, it's more often than not lust at first sight.'

'Such cynicism,' Lizzie sighed, 'and in one so young. The way you're going, you'll never meet anyone.'

'Yeah, well, I'd rather not meet anyone than meet the wrong one. There are a lot of weirdos out there, which the newspapers testify to all too often. And, anyway, twenty-seven is not that young,' she indignantly repudiated.

'Well, come for me then — ple-ease?'

'Oh, for heaven's sake,' Becca muttered. 'Speed dating? Really?'

'Yeah, really. It'll be exciting. Fun, even. You know, that thing we used to have. Look, you don't have to follow up on anything if you don't want to. They don't give out your home address on the evening. You'll be contacted with the phone numbers and email addresses of any interested parties. Both easily ignored, if that's what you want.' She eyed Becca pleadingly. 'Come on. We're stuck in a rut. It's time to climb out and experience life.'

In the end, as she invariably did, Becca gave in, simply to get a bit of peace and quiet. Lizzie wasn't one to give up on anything, and Becca knew she'd nag and nag until she got her own way, an ordeal she simply couldn't face.

And that was how she found herself walking into a large room in the only hotel that the town of Ashleigh Cross possessed, the Cross Hotel. Lizzie had already registered them both, so all they had to do was pay the fee for the evening.

They were greeted at the door and handed labels for each of them to wear. They also were given a sheet of paper with all the men's names written down. All they had to do was tick the name of anyone they wanted to meet again. They would have five minutes with each man and then a whistle would sound to signal it was time to move on.

Becca's heartbeat quickened as a trickle of dread crept through her. What the hell was she doing? Why had she let Lizzie talk her into such madness? She glanced around and saw a row of tables with chairs each side running the length of the room. She swallowed, tempted to take to her heels and leave. Especially when she realised that several of the men were staring at her, all of her, as well as at some of the other women still walking in. By the look in their eyes, she wouldn't be surprised if they weren't grading each of them, her included, with marks out of ten.

She swallowed again. It felt humiliating. 'I can't do this,' she muttered to Lizzie.

Lizzie reached out and grasped her arm. 'Yes, you can. Relax and just enjoy a new experience.'

From then on, things became a bit of a blur for Becca. She was aware of asking and being asked questions before gradually she felt herself relaxing, and found herself admitting that Lizzie was right — it was fun. So much fun, in fact, she ended up ticking three of the men's names.

Well,' Lizzie said as they walked back to Becca's car at the end of the event, 'what did you think?'

'That you were right. It was fun.'

'So how many did you tick? I did four.'

'Three,' Becca sheepishly admitted. 'Although whether they'll be as interested in me — ?' She shrugged.

However, a couple of evenings later, when she logged on to her inbox on her laptop, she found an email from the

5

organiser of the speed dating event, giving her the phone numbers and email addresses of the three men she'd been interested in.

She grinned, even as a shiver of misgiving edged through her. She wondered how Lizzie had got on. Before she could ring her friend, however, her own mobile phone rang. Unsurprisingly, it was Lizzie. A highly excited Lizzie, moreover.

'I've got two matches,' she cried without any sort of preliminary greeting. 'How many have you had?'

'Three.'

'See?' Lizzie chuckled. 'I told you. Are you going to contact them?'

'I-I'm not sure.' And she wasn't. All of a sudden, it felt too risky, she supposed. After all, she knew nothing about these men apart from what they'd told her on Wednesday evening, and that could all have been lies. Exaggerations at the very least. People tended to portray themselves in the best light.

But Lizzie wasn't about to let her get away with that. 'Not sure?' she cried. 'If it's the three I think it is, then they're all dead dishy. Especially the Italian-looking one. He watched you all evening, even when he was talking to me. Which I have to say, I found particularly hurtful.' She'd put on a deeply wounded tone, which Becca knew was completely false. Lizzie loved nothing better than playing games with people. 'Which, incidentally, is why I didn't tick him. I guessed I'd be onto a loser.'

'You mean Marco Vicente?'

'That's him. He was obviously very taken with you. Is he one of them?'

'Yes, but . . . well, he was a bit intense,' Becca murmured.

'What's wrong with intense, for heaven's sake? You should be flattered.'

'We-ell . . . '

'Oh, for God's sake, woman. Live a little. Enjoy it while you can. When was the last time a man, any man, looked at you like that?'

'Can't remember.' That wasn't true, however. One name in particular sprang to mind; she wasn't about to mention it to Lizzie, however. It was sure to provoke the sort of conversation she was keen to avoid.

'Exactly. So go for it. I mean, you can't blame the bloke. You did look gorgeous — but then you always do.' Lizzie sighed. 'It's that mane of wavy chestnut hair and those green eyes, the high cheekbones, that rose-tinted mouth.'

'Yeah, and the freckled nose, the wretched freckles that no amount of lemon juice would bleach out,' Becca grumbled, recalling her desperation as a teenager to remove what she'd viewed as deeply unattractive blemishes. They had faded a little over the past few years, but with the first rays of sun there they were, back again.

But Lizzie continued as if Becca hadn't spoken. 'And that's not taking into account your figure and those long, shapely legs.' She gave a heartfelt sigh. 'Let's face it, I'm no competition for all of that.'

'Oh, come on,' Becca said. 'I'd give my eye teeth for your silky smooth hair that does whatever you want it to, unlike my mop which rampages every which way however much lacquer I spray on it. Then there's your long neck, and your figure's lovely. Anyway, quite a few men spent a while gazing at you too.'

'Okay,' Lizzie retorted, 'enough of the mutual admiration. Again, I ask — are you going to get in touch with them?'

'I've only just had their details.'

'Well, I'm going to phone mine. There's no point in hanging around.'

'Hmm.' Becca was reluctant to do that. It felt too intimate, somehow. 'I'll probably email in the first instance. Or I might simply wait for them to contact me.'

'Chicken,' Lizzie mocked.

'Not really. I don't want to appear too eager, that's all.'

'Hmm. Good point,' Lizzie agreed.

'Playing hard to get can pay off. Oh, to hell with it — I'm going to phone. At the age of twenty-eight, I've got no time to waste.' And with that statement, she rang off.

Becca grinned to herself. She wished she had half the courage, the get-up-and-go that seemed to come so effortlessly to her friend. A soft meow sounded by the side of her.

'Hello, Queen Bee.' She lifted up her pet, a grey and white cat, and buried her face in the soft velvety fur. However, Bee wasn't having any of that. She wriggled herself free and leapt from Becca's arms, to land expertly on the floor and on all four feet, whereupon she stalked off into the corner of the room and proceeded to indulge in an energetic bout of personal hygiene.

Becca smiled. She'd always called her Queen Bee, right from the first time she'd seen her. That had been six months ago when she'd attached herself to Becca on her walk home from town, something she rarely did as her cottage lay at the end of a mile-long lane. With no collar or identity tag, Becca had assumed the animal was a stray and, viewing it as the hand of Fate — she'd been feeling somewhat lonely of late — had generously taken her in. The animal's bearing had been unmistakeably regal, and from that day on, the cat had moved around as if it were she who owned the cottage that Becca had purchased twelve months ago, her intention to renovate it a task she had yet to embark upon. But the truth was the longer she lived in it, the more she liked it as it was. It had personality, character. It was cosy, with its modest-sized low-beamed rooms and its wood-burning stove in the sitting room. Maybe come spring? It was late October now, and the dreary winter months that lay ahead weren't condu-cive to that sort of work.

She'd just settled herself in an armchair with a cup of coffee when her mobile phone rang. Lizzie, to tell her

11

how she'd got on? But when she looked at the screen, she saw that there was no number shown, just 'unknown caller'. Her heart leapt.

'H-hello,' she cautiously said.

'Is that Becca?' It was a man's voice.

'Yes. Who — ?'

'This is Marco Vicente.'

'Oh.' The single word was more of a soft sigh. Mainly because her heart was performing all sorts of uncomfortable leaps and bounds.

'I hope you don't mind me ringing you.'

'No, no, not at all. Heavens, no.' And now she was gushing, thereby sounding more like a teenager than a mature woman of twenty-seven. But the truth was, Marco had been her favourite of all the men she'd spoken to. Even so, she was glad he couldn't see her, because she could feel herself blushing, a girlish tendency she simply couldn't seem to rid herself of. It had embarrassed her many times over the past few years.

'I wondered.' He sounded as if he might be as nervous as her; strangely, that reassured her. 'Could we meet for a drink, maybe a meal?'

'A drink would be good.' She wasn't ready to extend the date to a long drawn-out meal. She wanted to meet him on a more casual basis first, assess how she felt about him, and more importantly how he felt about her. If she was to be just a one-night stand, which she suspected some of these dates turned out to be, then she needed to know that. She could then guard against any sort of premature emotional involvement.

'Tomorrow evening? Saturday?'

She could hear that he was smiling, which added to her sense of certainty that everything would be okay. And really, why not agree to meet him? It would be one evening out of the rest of her life. If she didn't like him, well, no harm done. She wouldn't see him again. And as Lizzie had stressed, there was no point in hanging around.

'I'd like that,' she said.

'Good. So, the White Hart, eight o'clock? We can have a drink and get to know each other a little better.'

Her thoughts exactly. This evidence of a shared sentiment boded well for the future: their feelings were completely in tune. 'That sounds great. I'll see you there.' Belatedly, there seemed everything to play for.

* * *

The next day, the remaining two men had also made contact. They'd decided to do it via email, which made it easier for Becca to prevaricate. She arranged to meet the first one, Gary Summers, on Monday evening, and the other one, Andy Gilmour, the following Monday.

But as the day wore on, Becca grew increasingly nervous and unsure about her evening's date with Marco, until by seven o'clock her stomach was under siege from a swarm of highly active butterflies.

She and Lizzie had arranged that they'd each phone the other halfway through the evening — Lizzie also had a date — in case either of them needed an excuse to make a quick getaway. Lizzie's was at the only other pub on the high street, the Green Frog.

As Becca changed her working outfit of black skirt and white blouse for a pair of trousers and a lightweight sweater, she asked herself, what if Marco turned out to be the sort of man she most disliked: arrogant, conceited, self-obsessed? With his good looks, he could well turn out to be exactly that. They'd only spent five minutes in each other's company, after all. She and Lizzie hadn't lingered once they'd had their time with each man. Eager to discuss the merits of the ones they'd selected to hopefully meet up with again, they'd sped off to the nearby Chinese restaurant for something to eat and a bottle of wine.

She wondered now, could she cancel the date? She had his mobile phone number. She was sorely tempted, but her sense of what was right overrode that. She'd agreed to meet him, so she had to go. At least she was driving herself there, so there was no risk of him escorting her home. It had seemed a sensible precaution. Her cottage was an isolated one, the nearest neighbour being at least half a mile away. It had formerly been a farm worker's home, which was why she'd initially decided its two rooms upstairs and two down-stairs needed renovation. A minute bathroom had been added at some point, and that was something that Becca did intend to extend into the next-door bedroom. It would make that room very small, more of a box room really; but as it was extremely unlikely she'd ever have visitors, a guest room wasn't a priority.

Both of her parents had been killed in a car accident ten years ago. She'd sold their home and gone to live with her grandmother; that was, until she had developed dementia eighteen months ago and was forced to move into a local care home, where she still resided. Becca had subsequently sold her house to fund the cost of the care, and then she'd used the remaining portion of her inheritance from her parents to purchase her cottage. Previously to that, she'd used a substantial sum to start up her own beauty salon, which she ran in partnership with Lizzie: the Pamper Parlour. They shared all the overheads, and so far it was working well. Lizzie was the hair stylist and Becca did the facials, manicures, and pedicures.

She stared at her reflection now in the mirror. Not bad. For once, even her wayward hair was behaving itself. Mind you, she had sprayed the better part of a can of lacquer onto it. She'd wanted to look especially good, because Marco was an extremely handsome man. Thirty-three years old and six feet tall, she'd estimated at the time of meeting, with hair the colour of a raven's wing, and dark brown eyes that had felt as if they were burning into her. His accent, although slight — he'd lived in the UK for the past twelve years, he'd told her — was as sexy as hell. He'd moved here on leaving full-time education in Italy in search of work. He now worked as manager of a large car salesroom in West Markham, a larger town than Ashleigh Cross just five miles away, selling high-end vehicles, mainly Jaguars and Range Rovers. He told her that he himself drove a Jaguar. She wondered now why he'd felt the need to attend a speed-dating event. She'd have thought he'd have women waiting in line to go out with him.

As she left the cottage — much to Queen Bee's disapproval, judging by the way she wound herself around Becca's ankles, at the same time loudly meowing — and climbed into her Polo, the butterflies once again made their presence felt. *For goodness sake,* she chided herself, *you're a twenty-seven-year-old woman, not an eighteen-year-old.*

She started up the engine and all too

quickly reached the high street, where she spent several minutes trying to locate a parking space. Once she did, she headed for the White Hart. It lay halfway along the street, sandwiched between a Tesco Express and a newsagent-cum-bookshop. She hesitated outside for a couple of minutes, bracing herself to go in. When she did so, a swift glance around revealed no sign of Marco. She checked her wristwatch. It was five past eight. Had he had second thoughts too? To her astonishment, a disconcerting mix of disappointment and relief pierced her. With the disappointment finally gaining the upper hand, she swung to leave, only to collide with him as he strode in.

'Becca, I'm late. I'm so sorry.' He reached for her as she staggered backwards, grasping her by the shoulders in order to steady her.

Becca took a deep breath. His touch had set her pulse racing madly. Jeez, she'd forgotten how good-looking he was. How charismatic. And she wasn't the only woman to think so, if the manner in which several others were staring at him, a couple of them with open mouths, was anything to go by.

'Please, forgive me?' As he spoke, he smiled at her. It illuminated his entire face, transforming him from merely good-looking into someone unbelievably handsome. The sort of handsome you saw on a cinema screen, and only rarely then.

After another deep breath, Becca felt herself melting, the blood catapulting round her body. And all she could think was, what on earth had this gorgeous man seen in her to make him ask to meet her again?

2

But he was undeniably seeing something now, because his glittering gaze roamed all over her before he bent forward, sliding an arm around her waist as he dropped a kiss upon her cheek. His lips lingered, soft and warm, his minty breath feathering her skin as he murmured, 'You look gorgeous. Thank you for agreeing to meet me.'

'Marco, fancy bumping into you. I don't often see you around these parts. Won't you introduce me?'

Becca swivelled her head and took a step backwards as Marco released his hold on her, only to find herself looking at yet another remarkably handsome man. Where had they both been hiding till now? Trying not to be too obvious about it, she scrutinised the stranger. There was something familiar about him. Maybe she'd noticed him as she'd walked about town? He'd be very hard to miss, after all.

'Well, I don't often come here,' Marco replied. 'I didn't realise you did.' He glanced at Becca then and said, 'Becca, meet Orlando Wheatley. Lando for short. Lando, meet Becca, short for Rebecca, Seymour.'

Lando Wheatley's gaze rested on Becca's face, a face that she could feel warming as the dreaded blush began its journey upwards. 'Nice to meet you, Rebecca.' Curiosity glittered in eyes that were the exact shade of wet slate as he cocked his head and examined her every bit as closely as she'd examined him. 'Have we met before?'

'I don't think so,' Becca managed to murmur, 'but I have lived here all my life, so . . . ' She shrugged. ' . . . maybe you've seen me around?' And it was then, in that split second, that she remembered exactly where she'd seen him before. She was amazed she could have forgotten.

She'd been eighteen, almost nineteen, at the time; he'd been older by five or six years, she'd estimated. She'd been struck instantly by his chiselled good looks, his height — six feet plus, his powerful build, and his unusual grey eyes. She'd also noticed his 'café au lait'-coloured hair, a lock of which had dropped over his forehead, just as it was doing now. But it had been his mouth that had really captured her attention. She recalled thinking how sensuous, sexy even, it had looked with its full lower lip.

They'd been at a party; he'd been standing with friends on the opposite side of the room from her, apparently engrossed in their conversation. Then, quite unexpectedly, he'd swivelled his head and caught her staring at him. A strange little gleam had appeared in his eye. Interest? she'd wondered with a lurch of her heart. Or something less flattering — amusement, maybe? As he'd glanced away again almost at once, she hadn't had the time to decide. She recalled how indignant she'd felt at his almost instantaneous — arrogant, even — dismissal of her, because she'd gone to a great deal of trouble with her outfit that evening. But now, with a flush of embarrassment, she remembered how short her skirt had been and how figure-revealing her tight sweater. She must have looked cheap. She'd never seen him again; hadn't even thought of him. And now here he was, large as life and standing right in front of her.

'Hmm. That could be it, but I'm sure our paths have crossed more closely at some time.' The grey eyes narrowed at her, darkening as he visibly speculated on where they might have come across each other. All Becca could do was pray he wouldn't recollect the occasion. She didn't want to be remembered as the tarty teenager in the figure-revealing outfit. 'How long have you and Marco known each other?'

'Not long.' She had no intention of revealing how she and Marco had met.

Marco raised an eyebrow at her as his

lips curved in a knowing smile. However, all he said was, 'I have every intention of putting that right, I can assure you.' His smile now was an intimate one, his glance warmly caressing.

Becca saw Lando's mouth tighten as what she interpreted as displeasure wreathed his handsome features. What was his problem? Did he not approve? Of her? Of Marco? Of their meeting? She wondered why not. Oh God, was Marco married? Was that it? Or was it that he'd recalled exactly where he'd seen her before? Determined not to be cowed by what she interpreted as disapproval, she returned his stare, mutely daring him to say any more. Even if Marco was married, what she and he did was none of Lando's business. Nor was how they had met. And nor, come to that, was what she'd chosen to wear all those years ago.

However, if he was indeed displeased by something, he gave no further indication of it. His tone was smooth, indifferent almost. 'Okay, well, have a good evening. Marco, we need to have a talk. Give me a call.' But his expression had hardened as he spoke directly to Marco, belying the cordiality of his words.

If Marco noticed this, he gave no sign. 'Certainly. Monday okay?'

'Fine. First thing, though. I've a busy day.' He glanced back at Becca. 'It's been nice meeting you, Rebecca.'

'Actually, it's Becca. I prefer it,' she brusquely told him.

A small smile flirted with the corners of his mouth. 'That's a shame. Rebecca is such a lovely name.'

That sounded dangerously like criticism. She frowned before glancing at Marco. He looked apprehensive, belatedly. She wondered why.

'I'll say goodbye then. Till Monday, Marco.' And with a cool smile, Lando Wheatley strode away — and out of her life for good, Becca hoped. She watched as he joined a woman on the other side

of the room. A very beautiful woman
— his wife?

'Come on.' Marco guided her in the
opposite direction to the one Lando
had taken, heading for an empty table
for two.

'So how do you know Lando?' she
asked. They hadn't looked like natural
friends. In fact, Lando had displayed an
authoritative attitude towards Marco, if
anything.

'He's my boss.'

Could that be why Marco had looked
so apprehensive? She suspected Lando
Wheatley would be a demanding
employer. When Marco didn't elaborate
on his abrupt statement, Becca went
on, 'Who's that with him? His wife?
She's very beautiful. Do they live
hereabouts?'

Marco didn't at first answer. Then,
'You seem very interested in him. Have
you met him before? He seemed to
think he knew you.' His gaze had
narrowed with what looked like suspicion.

Becca decided to be honest. She had nothing to hide; it had been a fleeting encounter, nothing more. They hadn't even spoken. In fact, she was astonished that Lando had remembered — well, not remembered precisely, but clearly something about her had struck a chord within him.

'Well, not met as such. I remember seeing him once, that's all, eight or nine years ago. It's just idle curiosity.'

'Hmm.' She wasn't sure he believed her. But as he then went on to smile warmly at her and say, 'No, she isn't his wife,' she decided she must be imagining things. 'I've no idea who she is. He's not married. Resolutely single, as a matter of fact. So if you're keen to alter his status, don't waste your time.' He was almost sneering now, whether at her or Lando's bachelordom, she couldn't have said. 'You add to that the fact that he's very much a ladies' man.' He shrugged and, as if keen to change the subject, asked, 'What do you want to drink? I'll go and get it.'

'I'll have a red wine, please. Merlot if possible.'

Marco strode to the bar. Becca watched him go. He was a bit touchy on the subject of Lando Wheatley. She glanced across the room towards him and his lovely companion. He sounded exactly what she would have expected him to be: self-assured to the point of arrogance. However, when he suddenly swivelled his head and stared back at her, she quickly looked away; not before she'd noticed the self-satisfied smile that flirted with his mouth, however. Huh. As she'd already concluded, and moreover had concluded the first time she'd seen him, he was supremely convinced of his appeal to women. Well, he could think again if he believed she was in any way attracted to him.

So she was more than a little mortified when she found herself stealing another glance at him. This time, however, he didn't notice. Nonetheless, she was relieved when Marco returned, and even more relieved when half an hour later Lando and his companion left.

'So,' Marco said as he took his seat again, 'tell me all about yourself. Five minutes is nowhere long enough to exchange life histories.' He grinned invitingly at her.

'Well, I don't know about my life history, or how interesting you'll find it . . .' But, nonetheless, she proceeded to tell him about her parents and their accident, how she'd lived with her grandmother before her move into a care home, and finally her possible plans for her cottage and her future at her salon, hoping throughout that what she was fearing had been a veritable monologue; that she wasn't boring him rigid.

However, she couldn't have been, because he instantly asked with what sounded like genuine interest, 'So are you your own boss?'

'Yes.'

'Isn't that a great deal of responsibility?'

'I share it with my best friend, Lizzie. We work together in partnership.'

'Oh yes, I remember her. She came with you to the speed-dating event.' He eyed her. 'So where is this Pamper Parlour?'

'Do you know the row of shops on Green Street? We rent the one between the flower shop and a small general store.'

'I know it, yes.' Something flickered in his eye then. 'Lando recently bought that block. Did you know?'

'No. We only received notification of a change of ownership a few days ago.' She frowned. 'So Wheatley Enterprises is Lando?' She hadn't immediately realised that, not even when she'd heard his name. She wasn't usually that slow to put two and two together. She must have been too preoccupied in trying to remember where she'd seen him before.

'Yes. Have you heard about his plans?'

'Plans?'

'Yeah.'

'No, I haven't. Presumably you have?'

'Yes. He wants to renovate all the frontages, make them look more upmarket; his words, not mine. After which, he intends to raise the rents.'

Becca was dumbstruck. She and Lizzie could barely afford the rent as it was. A rise would swallow up what little profit they made.

'You look shocked,' Marco said.

'I am. I'm pretty sure the other tenants haven't heard anything about this. Did Lando tell you?'

'Not him personally, no. But someone in the know did. I'm pretty sure the info is reliable. You'll probably be getting a letter about it any day soon.'

'Oh God,' Becca groaned. 'We can only just afford the rent as it is. And I have to say, the place really isn't worth any more. It's not in a prime position, after all, being on the edge of town.'

'You could always register your protest with him. I can give you his email address and phone number.'

'Could you?'

'Sure. Hang on. I'll write them down for you. His landline at head office, his mobile number, and his email address.' He was scribbling it all down on a small notepad as he spoke. He then tore out the sheet of paper and gave it to her. 'It might be better to use the email address and put everything in writing.' He looked belatedly anxious then. 'Don't mention it came from me, will you? It could cost me my job.'

'I won't.' She scanned the details on the sheet of paper, resolving to email Lando Wheatley first thing Monday morning, trusting he wouldn't put two and two together and come up with the truth about her informant. Maybe she should wait a week or two? Only to immediately decide that the sooner she registered her protest at his plans, the better.

Although the disturbing news that Marco had given her continued to play on her mind, she did manage to enjoy herself. Marco proved to be a charming companion, knowledgeable, and with a pronounced sense of humour. So at the end of the evening, when he asked if they could meet again on the following Saturday evening, she had no hesitation in agreeing.

The next two dates would have large shoes to fill. Too large? She was tempted to cancel them both, but then decided that would be rude. And who knew — one of them could turn out to be even more of a match for her.

She rang Lizzie when she got home. The prearranged phone calls had proved unnecessary, but even so, she wanted to hear how her friend had got on.

'How did it go?' Becca asked.

'Not bad, not bad at all. We've fixed a second date. How about you?'

'The same. He was great, good company.'

But Lizzie didn't let her finish. 'Sam's just rung me. He spotted you and Marco leaving the pub as he was driving by. Actually — ' She paused as if unsure whether to go on or not. ' — he's been seeing someone for a while now. The trouble is — ' She paused again. ' — I get the impression he's still keen on you. I-I didn't tell him about the speed dating. I suspect he wouldn't approve.'

Becca didn't see what it had to do with Sam. He was Lizzie's older brother, and he and Becca had dated for a while. But as far as Becca was concerned, it hadn't felt right, mainly because she'd known him almost as long as she'd known Lizzie. As a consequence, he felt like more of a brother than a potential lover. Things fortunately hadn't progressed that far, mainly due to Becca's reluctance to take things any further than a warm friendship. When she'd decided to end it, she'd made every effort to let him down gently, but she'd known she'd hurt him. However, that had been a couple of years ago now. He should have got over her rejection by this time. Still, if he was seeing someone else, that was a good sign.

'I haven't actually met her yet,' Lizzie went on. 'He seems reluctant to introduce her to me; don't know why. The trouble is, I think he measures everyone against you. He doesn't say a lot, or even mention you much anymore; it's just a feeling I have.'

'I'm sorry, Lizzie, but it simply didn't feel right. I wonder — are you sure you're not imagining it all; projecting your own hopes onto him? I know you were keen for us to make a go of things.'

'No, I know it's not going to happen. But you're right, I did have hopes of you becoming my sister-in-law.' She sounded wistful now. 'Anyway, I'll see you on Monday.'

Becca decided not to repeat what Marco had told her about Lando Wheatley's plans for the salon; not yet. She'd check that he had things right first. There was no point in worrying Lizzie prematurely.

Come Monday morning, and before going to the salon, Becca emailed Lando Wheatley asking if the rumour she'd heard about the renovations of the shop frontages was correct; and, as a consequence of that, was he intending to raise the rents? Resolving to keep things on a professional basis, she signed herself as Rebecca Seymour of the Pamper Parlour, all the while wondering if he'd remember her name.

Given the speed of his response and his opening sentence, 'Good to hear from you, Rebecca,' she assumed he did. He went on, 'I am looking into these matters, yes, but as yet no firm decision has been taken. I'd very much like to hear your views on the matter, as one of my much valued tenants. Perhaps we could meet at the White Hart this evening at eight o'clock. Can you let me know if this is agreeable? I'll be in the office until eleven a.m. Yours, Lando Wheatley.'

Becca wasted no time in replying: 'I'm sorry, but I'm afraid this evening isn't possible. I have another commitment. How about tomorrow, Tuesday, same time?'

Again, he instantly replied: 'That's fine. If I don't hear otherwise, I'll expect you at eight.'

Becca drove to the salon, and her day went as every other day did. She was kept busy, as was Lizzie. So busy that they barely had time to talk to each other, which ensured that the last thing Becca felt like doing that evening was going out on her date with Gary Summers. They'd also agreed to meet at the White Hart. However, the second she spotted him, she conceded he had no chance of rivalling Marco. She hadn't remembered him as being a little overweight, although to his credit, he was immaculately dressed and perfectly groomed with dark well-cut hair, and dressed in a smart jacket and trousers. His brown eyes lit up with admiration as she approached him. He got to his feet, and she saw he was also shorter than she'd realised. Or was she being too critical now, comparing him so unfavourably with Marco?

'Becca,' he said, 'how lovely to see you again.'

'Gary,' she murmured, taking the other seat at the table. Her glance fleetingly took in the other people in the room, half-expecting to spot Lando again. Her disappointment when she didn't surprised and dismayed her. However, she did spot Sam. He was with a woman. She must be the one Lizzie had mentioned. She was very pretty. Well, good luck to him, she decided. Maybe he'd found the right one, who knew? He saw her and gave her a thumbs-up, along with a warm smile. Becca smiled back and gave a small wave, deciding that Lizzie was way out with her suspicion that he was still hankering after her if the way he was looking at his companion was anything to go by, and she rather thought it was.

Gary noticed her sideways glance and smile at Sam and asked somewhat waspishly, 'Do you know him?'

'Yes, he's the brother of my friend, Lizzie. She was at the speed dating with me.'

He looked relieved. 'Oh, I see. For a minute there I thought I had a serious rival.'

Becca regarded him in astonishment. 'Gary, this is our first meeting.'

'Not quite our first,' he murmured.

'Our first real meeting, and it's a bit premature to be talking about a serious rival, isn't it?'

He gave a snort of what she took to be amusement. 'Of course it is; much too early. I was only joking.' He indicated the bottle of white wine that sat on the table along with two glasses. 'I've done the honours. I know how you ladies like your white vino.' And he gave another snort of amusement.

'Actually, Gary, I prefer red.' Dear God, if this was how the evening was set to continue, with him high-handedly

40

making decisions on her behalf, she couldn't imagine it being much of a success.

He looked genuinely dismayed at that. 'Oh, dear.'

Becca immediately felt a stab of remorse. 'It's okay, I'll drink it.' She pushed her empty glass towards him.

But after such a shaky start, it wasn't surprising that the evening didn't progress well. Conversation was stilted, and she couldn't help comparing him to Marco and surprisingly to Lando. So, when after a mere hour or so, she told him she had to go and he asked to see her again, she replied, 'I'm all booked up for the next few weeks, Gary. Can I email you sometime?'

An odd expression crossed his face at that. It was almost a sneer. However, all he said was, 'Sure. I've got a few other dates lined up as well, but then, that was the point of it all, wasn't it?'

Becca couldn't get away fast enough. She had to pass just a few feet away from Sam and his date, but he didn't seem to notice her. He was clearly enjoying himself as he laughed at something that his companion had said. Feeling hugely reassured by this evidence that he was getting on with his life, she had no hesitation in stopping and saying, 'Hi, how are you, Sam? Good to see you. It's been a while. Won't you introduce me?'

Sam smiled up at her, seemingly untroubled at having seen her a second time, and with a different man to boot. 'Of course. This is Mel. Mel, meet Bex, a close friend of my sister's — and me, of course.' He gave a chuckle. 'We actually dated for a while, didn't we, Bex?'

Mel beamed up at Becca and thrust out a hand.' So nice to meet you. That's an unusual name, Bex. What's it short for?'

'Rebecca. But everyone — except Sam, that is — calls me Becca.'

Sam then asked, 'Had a good evening? You seem to be getting around a bit. I saw you with someone else on

. . . Saturday, wasn't it?' Becca nodded. 'Still, there's nothing like a bit of variety, is there?'

'They're just friends.' She eyed him. Was that sarcasm she detected? Or was he merely amused? She hoped it was the latter.

'Well, good for you. But maybe you need to be careful. People will have you down as a flirt. Two different men in as many evenings.'

Stung by what definitely sounded like criticism, she tartly replied, 'They can think what they like, Sam.' She only just stopped herself from adding, 'As can you.' Instead, she said, 'It's my life, after all.'

'Quite right, too,' he murmured. He looked around the room, clearly searching for Gary. 'Had a good time? Although it didn't last long.'

Becca pulled a face and said, 'I've had better evenings,' before turning her head as she sensed someone behind her and saw Gary. Damn. He must have crept up behind her. But surely Sam would have seen him? Had he deliberately allowed her to be indiscreet? Surely not. Sam was usually the kindest of men, always watching out for her and Lizzie in their younger days. He'd never exhibited the slightest indication of spite, not even when she'd ended things between them. He'd been upset, true, but not spiteful, or even resentful.

She felt her face warming. She'd been rude, even though that hadn't been her intention. She'd put her carelessness down to the couple of glasses of wine she'd drunk.

However, if Gary had overheard her, he gave no sign of it. He simply smiled at her and said, 'I'll see you around.'

'Yeah, sure,' she responded, relief bestowing a lilt to her tone.

Saying her goodbyes to Sam and Mel, she left the pub and swiftly made her way back to her car, feeling distinctly more optimistic about Sam's love life. As usual, Lizzie had exaggerated everything. He certainly wasn't moping over her. He and Mel had looked very happy in each other's company. She'd make sure she told Lizzie that, trusting it would put an end to any future speculation about the possibility of her and Sam getting back together.

*   *   *

The next evening arrived far too quickly for Becca, with the result that she felt edgy and nervous, and totally unprepared for the meeting with Lando. She'd tried to marshal her thoughts in order to present a well-planned and plausible reason for him not to raise their rent, but aside from the obvious ones, she didn't have a lot of success. She'd have to play it by ear.

The one thing that buoyed her was the fact that he'd agreed so readily to meet her. It indicated that he must be prepared to listen to her argument. But if it should turn out that he was determined to go ahead with things, then she'd have to get the other tenants on side in order to come up with some sort of plan to effectively oppose him. Because there must be others amongst them who would find it difficult to pay more rent and survive as a profitable business.

3

By the time Becca arrived, Lando was already seated at a table on the far side of the lounge of the White Hart, reading a newspaper and sipping from what looked like a glass of beer. As a consequence, he didn't see her until she was standing right in front of him.

He glanced up and with a smile said, 'Good evening.' Then he folded the paper and got to his feet. 'Good of you to come. Please — ' He indicated the seat opposite him. ' — sit down.'

Becca did as he said, still without saying a word.

'Now, what can I get you to drink?'

'A glass of red wine, please.'

'Any in particular?'

'Merlot will be fine, thanks.'

Within seconds, it seemed, he was back and placing a very large glass of wine in front of her. She regarded it dubiously. Was he hoping to get her drunk and thereby persuade her to agree to his plans? She wouldn't put such an intention past him. In fact, she wouldn't put much at all past him.

He took his own seat again; his gaze, as it rested on her, a level one. There was no indication of any sort of concern over what she might have to say. He was clearly confident he'd get his own way, whether she was intoxicated or not. A result she was sure he was accustomed to obtaining. After all, he'd been immediately served at the bar — no waiting in a queue for Lando Wheatley. She felt her indignation growing. Well, he wasn't going to achieve what he wanted so easily with her. No, sir.

'Right,' he said. 'So tell me exactly what you've heard.'

'That you plan to renovate the frontages of all the shops in Green Street, one of which is mine.'

'Which one?'

'The Pamper Parlour.'

'Ah, yes. I know it.'

'And as a consequence of that, raise the rents. I don't know whether you realise how little profit we make on that road. It would be quickly swallowed up by higher rents, which could well put several of us, if not all of us, out of business.'

He tilted his head to one side as he continued to scrutinise her. 'Did you get this from Marco?' His eyes narrowed.

Her heart lurched. She didn't want to place Marco's job in jeopardy. She knew she should have waited a few days before emailing him. So why hadn't she? 'Of course not.' She hated having to lie, but she had no choice in the matter. She just hoped he believed her. 'I-I don't actually remember who mentioned it.' She'd never been a good liar. Her expression always gave her away, just as it probably was now. In desperation, she buried her face in her glass and took a large gulp of wine, only to promptly swallow the wrong way and start to choke.

Lando was still watching her closely; suspiciously, even. However, it didn't stop him from asking, 'Are you all right? Do you want me to . . . ' He got to his feet, clearly his intention being to come round to her and try to assist her.

Unable to talk, Becca waved him away. The last thing she wanted was to have Lando Wheatley hitting her on the back in the middle of a busy pub. She couldn't think of anything worse. Thankfully he sat back down, but he was frowning as he watched her struggle for breath.

Eventually, she managed to calm herself and she muttered, 'Sorry. Went the wrong way.'

'Well if you're okay, then to return to the subject of your salon . . . parlour . . . whatever. I haven't notified any of the tenants of my plans, mainly because the decision still has to be made. But I really do feel that if the shops are smartened up, it will increase business for you all. It is a rather rundown area.'

'Rundown?' Becca indignantly cried. 'It's not rundown. They just need a lick of paint.'

'They need a good deal more than that,' he bluntly said. 'The fascia boards are shabby and in most cases rotten; they need replacing. My plan is to have the same design and format for all of them; do it in one continuous length across all the shops. It would look a damn sight more stylish than the way it is now, a mishmash of different designs and colours. The windows would also be replaced, doors the same.'

'And what are we to do while this — this renovation work is being carried out?' she demanded.

'Carry on as usual,' he smoothly told her. 'It shouldn't prove too much of an inconvenience.'

'Oh, really? So it won't inconvenience our customers to have to navigate their way around workmen up ladders, pick their way through broken glass, avoid touching any wet paint?'

'It wouldn't be for long. The benefits

would be that you'd almost certainly attract many more customers. The shops would be eye-catching, encouraging people to stop instead of continuing on to the high street, thereby bringing in a lot more clients for you all. More passing trade, in other words.'

'Would it, now? And how much would this eye-catching renovation cost us, the tenants, in the form of higher rents? Because someone has to pay for it.' She lowered her voice to a murmur. 'And I can't imagine it being you.'

He must have decided to ignore her last few words, although she'd bet all she possessed that he'd heard them, because all he went on to say was, 'Nothing's been decided, as I've said.'

Becca began to get to her feet. 'Well, maybe when you *have* decided, you'll tell the people who are going to be the ones who actually pay for it all.'

He also got to his feet. 'Rebecca . . .'

'Everyone calls me Becca. I prefer it,' she snapped.

'Okay, Becca. Please, sit down. Let's

discuss this calmly, rationally.'

Her chest swelled as outrage engulfed her. 'Are you suggesting I'm being irrational?'

She'd noticed the way his gaze dropped to her breasts as they filled out her sweater. Okay, it had been the briefest of glances, but nevertheless, her sense of outrage deepened. Huh! Typical man. She glared at him as his eyes met hers once more. He did have the grace to look slightly embarrassed.

'No, I didn't mean it the way it sounded. But — please, sit down. Nothing's been decided.'

She did as he asked. 'Well, I'll warn you now. If you decide to go ahead with it all, I can assure you, you'll have a fight on your hands.'

A glimmer of amusement lit his grey eyes at that, as the corners of his mouth twitched. 'From all ten of you, presumably?' Now he was laughing at her. Not obviously, but it was there — in the twinkle of his eye, the subtle widening of his mouth, as if he were struggling to constrain his laughter.

Thoroughly incensed by this time, Becca retaliated. 'It might not sound like many to you, but you'll be surprised by what we can do.'

'Like what, exactly?' he quietly asked.

'Well . . . ' That stumped her. She hadn't spoken to any of the other tenants yet, so had no idea of their views on the matter. 'I-I'm sure we'll think of something.' God, how feeble was that? She should have prepared some sort of statement of intent; something with a bit more detail than 'I'm sure we'll think of something.' No wonder he was trying not to laugh. This observation was borne out by the more pronounced gleam of amusement that he was now making no attempt to disguise, that and the one raised eyebrow as he regarded her.

'Oh, you think it's funny, do you?' Becca ground the words out. 'To take the wrecking ball to people's livelihoods purely for profit?'

'No, I don't, and I wouldn't describe

what I've just outlined as taking a wrecking ball to people's livelihoods. Have you actually asked the other tenants what they think about the plans?'

Oh God, he'd sussed her out. He knew she had no plan of campaign. 'Well n-no, not yet. I-I wanted to hear what you had to say first before worrying everyone else. But I know that not one of them makes a huge profit, certainly not enough to absorb a large rent rise and stay solvent.'

All traces of amusement had vanished. Lando's slaty gaze had belatedly turned into a steely one. 'So in that case, I suggest you ask them. I'll write to them all, outlining my plans.'

'That's another thing,' she burst out. 'You'll need planning permission, surely, for such extensive alterations.'

'Yes, I will. That's all in hand.'

'Hah! I'm sure it is,' she scoffed. 'But whose hand is it in? Know someone in the planning department, do you?'

His mouth twisted in contempt at

that question. Becca's heart gave a gigantic heave. Oh God, her and her big mouth. She'd all but accused him of corruption. How would that help her case to strengthen her argument? Would she never learn? The times she'd landed herself in trouble . . .

'I'll pretend I didn't hear that,' he grimly said.

'S-sorry, that came out wrong.'

'Did it, now?' He clearly didn't believe her. He knew she'd meant every word. 'I'd be very careful what you say, and to whom, if I were you. I meant that I've already applied for planning permission.'

'I thought you hadn't decided,' she blurted.

'I haven't,' he smoothly replied, 'but I'm a great believer in being prepared.'

'I bet you were in the Boy Scouts,' she muttered.

'I was, actually. Dib, dib, did, and all that.' Amusement had once more replaced the steel in his eyes. It turned them from the colour of slate to that of blackberries, and it enhanced his good looks to something that was beyond breathtaking.

Somehow Becca managed to control her grin, mainly by biting firmly on her lower lip. Of course he saw her battle against laughter, and as a result, his gaze warmed even more. All of a sudden, he didn't appear quite so intimidating. In fact, he was beginning to seem likable.

He reinforced this impression by suggesting, 'Let's talk about something else. I promise to keep you fully informed about what's happening.' And much to Becca's annoyance, she found herself doing just that when he drawled, 'So tell me about yourself. Have you always lived in Ashleigh Cross? Because I'm positive I've seen you somewhere before, a few years ago.'

'You have. At a party, eight or nine years ago.'

'I knew it. I recognised you.'

'Did you?'

'Oh yes,' he murmured. 'Once seen,

never forgotten — in both of our cases, evidently.' There was a maddening knowing look to him now; a confident look. He'd realised she'd been attracted to him.

Becca couldn't prevent the rush of blood to her face. And damn him, he noticed that too.

'So you never moved away, then?'

'No. I lost my parents in a car accident when I was nineteen — just a few months after that party, as a matter of fact.'

His frown now was one of concern. 'My God. I'm so sorry. What did you do?'

'I went to live with my gran until fairly recently. She developed dementia and is now in a care home. Birchfield House. So I bought myself a small cottage in Willow Lane. Honeysuckle Cottage.'

'I know it. It's a bit isolated, isn't it? Or do you live with someone?'

'No, I'm on my own, but I like it like that. It was a farm worker's cottage and needs some work doing on it, although I'm rethinking that at the moment.'

'A good buy, was it?'

'It was. But if I do decide to go ahead with the renovations, it will have used up most of my inheritance from my parents.' She grimaced wryly. 'The sale of Gran's house is funding her care, so at least I don't have to worry about that.'

'I could put you in touch with a couple of good all-round men. They can turn their hands to anything, and they're not expensive. I'll email you their names if you like.'

'Thank you.' She knew she sounded surprised, but she couldn't help herself. The last thing she'd expected from this man was an offer of help.

He eyed her, his head cocked to one side. 'I'm not all bad, you know,' he softly said.

Deciding it was her turn to ask the questions, she went on, 'Where do you live?'

'Well, I only recently returned from

London, where I spent the last several years starting up my business, Wheatley Enterprises. I returned about eight months ago. I also had interests here. The car showroom, for instance, which Marco runs.' His expression darkened for a moment. It was as if he wanted to ask a question. She prayed it wouldn't be whether it had been Marco who'd told her of his plans. He must have had second thoughts, though, because he went on to say, 'Anyway, I bought Ashleigh House six months ago. Like Honeysuckle Cottage, it needs work done on it.'

Becca knew Ashleigh House. It was a massive place a mile or so out of town, on the opposite side to where she lived. She'd heard it had been sold but not to whom. It had gone for a price in the region of two and a half million pounds, or so rumour had it.

'You'll have to come and have a look at it. See what you think.'

She couldn't resist asking, 'Why?'

He shrugged, drawing her gaze to the

width of his shoulders beneath the sweater he was wearing. He looked very fit. 'Just out of interest. You could maybe make a few suggestions, or even get a few ideas for your own cottage.'

She snorted. 'I don't think that what you'll be doing will be right for my place. You could fit my entire house into just one of your rooms, I imagine,' she finished drily. 'Don't you have an interior designer?'

'Not at the moment, but the way things are going I may have to resort to that. The thing is, I want it to be a home, not some sort of showplace.'

'Isn't there a . . . ' She hesitated. She didn't want to show too much interest in him. He might read it wrong. ' . . . woman in your life? The woman you were with the other evening, say?'

'Oh, no. Nina's just a friend. I did live with someone in London for a while, but we each had different ideas about things, so it didn't work out. There's been no one since.' He looked directly at her. 'Why? Are you applying for the position?'

'What? Certainly not,' she riposted. Really. What a preposterous question.

'The notion that bad, is it?'

'Well no. That is, I'm not looking for anyone.'

'So what's Marco, then?'

'A friend. I've only recently met him.' She certainly wasn't about to tell him about the speed-dating evening. She could just imagine the sarcastic comments that would provoke.

'Are you seeing him again?'

It was Becca's turn to stare at him now. 'Yes. Next Saturday, as a matter of fact.' Why was he so keen to know her plans? He couldn't really be interested in her, could he?

'You know he's a bit of a flirt, don't you?'

'I can deal with that. I'm a big girl now.' Maybe she should tell him that Marco had said much the same thing about him. She thought better of it, however. She didn't want to land Marco in even more trouble than he could already be in if Lando ever found out it was him who'd told her about his plans for the row of shops.

'So there's no one serious in your life?'

'Not at the moment, no.'

'How about if I show an interest?'

'You?' Her eyes widened at him.

'Yes.'

'Why?'

'I like you. I find you interesting. A bit different to the usual run-of-the-mill women.'

What the hell did that mean?

'You have spirit, ambition, and you're not afraid to voice your opinion. I like that.'

'Nothing to do with you trying to butter me up over your plans for the shops?'

He stiffened. 'Do you have so little confidence in your own attractiveness? But more than that, I find the fact that you actually believe me capable of such cold-blooded, devious behaviour insulting.' His features now resembled a block of granite, so bleak and chiselled they could well have been carved from the stone. It made his earlier steely look seem mild in comparison,

Oh good Lord, she'd done it again — allowed her wayward tongue free rein. She stared nervously at him. He looked about ready to kill her. She cringed back in her seat, away from him. 'I-I didn't mean that.'

'Then what did you mean? Please enlighten me.'

'Well, why would a man like you be interested in someone like me? I hardly move in your sort of circles.'

Splinters of ice crackled in his voice as he demanded, 'Why would you think I'd care about something like that?'

She shrugged. She really had no answer this time — a rarity for her, she mutely conceded.

'I've just told you I like you. I'm attracted to you. I believe we could share something good. Are those enough reasons?'

Becca stumbled to her feet. Now

would be a good time to leave. She didn't have any answers for him. But apart from that, she found it impossible to believe he was serious. He must be playing some kind of game with her. A game of tactics. 'No. I'm sorry. I'm too busy with my salon to have any sort of serious relationship.'

'Does Marco know that?' he roughly demanded.

'I've no idea. We've only met once.'

'But you plan to meet him again, or so you told me. If I were you, I'd tell him. He's not a man to be toyed with. He has quite a temper.'

She stared at him in dismay. 'What does that mean?'

'What it sounds like. He's of Italian descent, full of Mediterranean passion. Work it out for yourself.'

'I will. Thanks for the warning. I'll be off now. Please let me know as soon as you've made your decision about the shops.' If she sounded sarcastic, she didn't care. The fact was, Lando Wheatley was the very last man she'd get involved with. He'd only ever be out for himself, she was sure. If what Marco had told her was true, he'd pick her up, use her and then drop her again. Because whatever he said, she really wasn't his type. Maybe that was the attraction — she was the complete opposite of the women he usually dated.

Yet doubt lingered. For all her disagreement, anger even, over his intentions for her salon, she didn't think he was someone who would deliberately lie. What was more, he was clearly concerned about her seeing the other man. She frowned as she walked towards the exit door. What if he was right about Marco? And if she carried on seeing him, what would she be getting herself into?

4

One thing Becca did know — she needed to tell Lizzie about the possibility of renovations to the shop frontage before any letter arrived from Wheatley Enterprises. If she discovered that Becca had known and not told her, there'd be trouble. Lizzie had quite a temper at times, as Becca had found out to her cost more than once.

So as soon as Lizzie arrived at the salon the next morning, Becca took her into the small back room that they used for their coffee breaks and lunches, and related all that she knew so far. She'd had a close look at the front of Pamper Parlour as well as the other nine shops and had been forced to acknowledge that Lando was right — they did all need a more modern look.

However, Lizzie almost immediately

lived up to Becca's fears. 'Why am I not surprised?' were her first angry words before she went on to rant, 'I've heard all about Orlando Wheatley. Only out for himself. A ruthless entrepreneur, by all accounts. He's accumulated a fortune by buying up ailing companies and 'restructuring' them by forced redundancies, then selling them on for huge profits.'

'Well, I don't think he's quite that bad,' Becca protested.

'Take it from me, he is. We need to tell the others,' Lizzie went on. 'Warn them. Maybe we could get some sort of protest going.'

'That's what I originally thought. But have you had a good look at the fronts? Maybe Lando's — '

'Lando?' Lizzie echoed. 'Have you met him?'

Becca nodded, slightly sheepishly it had to be said.

'And you're on sufficiently intimate terms to call him Lando? Did he tell you about these plans?'

'Firstly, I'm not on any sort of terms with Lando Wheatley, and definitely not intimate ones. Marco told me — but that's strictly between you and me. He works for Lando, and it could land him in a great deal of trouble if Lando found out he'd told me. I-I emailed Lando with my concerns, and he asked to meet. So I agreed, intending to voice those concerns.'

Lizzie stared at her. 'And did you? Voice those concerns?'

'I did.'

'And?'

'And he told me it's not a done deal yet and he'd keep me informed of any decision.'

'Where did you meet?' Lizzie looked more intrigued now than angry.

'At the White Hart.'

'How cosy. He talked you round, did he?'

'No. I raised the matter of higher rents, and he argued that smarter frontages would generate more business for us all — which, I have to say, it probably would. I mean, have you had a good look at the fronts? They're very shabby; the wood's completely rotten in places. It wouldn't exactly inspire anyone to come in.'

'He *has* talked you round.' Lizzie's tone was heavy with disapproval. 'Mind you, I've heard he's extremely handsome.'

'That's got nothing to do with it,' Becca sharply retaliated.

Lizzie said nothing, simply raised a sceptical eyebrow.

'Really, it hasn't.'

'Methinks the lady doth protest too much,' Lizzie softly and probably not totally accurately quoted.

'What does that mean?' Becca hotly demanded.

'Nothing. Anyway, I say we should get a protest up and running before it's definite. Who knows — it might even halt the plans before they get started. In other words, stop him in his greedy tracks. I'll go and talk to the others, see what they think. If they think there's going to be a substantial rent hike, they'll be bound to agree.'

'We-ell, I'm not sure. I think we ought to wait and see.'

But she was talking to thin air. Lizzie had gone, raring to go, obviously. Becca sighed. She'd leave her to it. Her first appointment for a facial would be here any minute, so she began laying out the items she'd need.

Lizzie's first client arrived ten minutes later. 'Have a seat,' Becca invited. 'Lizzie won't be long.'

A couple of minutes later, Lizzie rushed back in. She politely assured her client she'd be with her in a couple of moments, then said, 'Becca, have you got a minute?'

Becca excused herself to her lady and followed Lizzie into the backroom. 'Well?'

'Everyone's as concerned as me. Not so much about the renovations, but certainly about the rent rise. No one can afford it, not right now.'

'Did you explain how the smarter

fronts would probably generate more business?'

'Yes, and they weren't impressed. Bob in the paper shop put it rather well, I thought. Wheatley Enterprises are expecting us to foot the bill for them. And frankly, that's not on.'

As that was a point she herself had made to Lando, Becca asked, 'So what's the plan then?'

'We refuse to allow them to do it. We hinder them every step of the way. For starters, try and stop the planning permission being granted.'

'Easier said than done. He already applied a while ago, I think. It might have been passed by now.'

'Hmmm.' Lizzie looked thoughtful. 'We'll have to come up with something to prevent work being started, then.'

'How do you propose to do that? Set up camp on the pavement? Stage a sit-in — or rather, a sit-out?' She tried to introduce a note of humour into things. It didn't work.

'You're on his side, aren't you?'

'No. Well, not really. I can see his point of view. What I can't see is how we'll stop him; prevent the alterations.'

'We get up a petition,' Lizzie cried. 'Ask our clients to sign it.'

'Why would they do that? It won't affect them.'

'Of course it will, if we explain we'll have to put our prices up to cover the rent rise.'

'True, but still . . . ' She nibbled at her bottom lip.

'Or we simply stop paying rent at all. See how he likes that.'

'For heaven's sake, he'll take us all to court for non-payment. Either that, or he'll just evict us.'

'Mmm.' Lizzie now also looked doubtful. 'Can he do that? We have a lease.'

'I imagine that if we refuse to pay, he can. Look, let's wait and see what happens. Nothing's been decided. He may not go ahead with it all. We don't want to antagonise him needlessly.'

Grudgingly, Lizzie agreed, and Becca

returned to her by this time more-than-a-little-tetchy client.

* * *

The remainder of the week mercifully passed without incident. None of the other nine tenants seemed prepared to take any sort of action against Lando. There were a lot of heated words exchanged, but not very much more. There were no words from Lando either. Everything seemed to be suspended in a worrying limbo.

By the time Saturday evening arrived, Becca was eager to get out of the cottage to go and meet Marco. He'd rung her the evening before and suggested they have a meal, this time at an Italian restaurant run by a friend of his. Becca readily agreed.

'I'll pick you up,' he'd offered.

But Becca wasn't ready for that, so she said, 'No, it's fine. I'd rather come under my own steam.' The truth was she didn't want to place herself in the position of having to invite him into her home at the end of the evening. Lando's warning about him had lingered. Anyway, she knew where the restaurant was — in the next village to Ashleigh Cross, smack in the middle of the high street. It would only take her five minutes to drive there.

It actually took over ten, almost fifteen, due to road repairs and temporary traffic lights, but fortunately she managed to find a car parking space almost at once. Still, she was out of breath by the time she dashed into the restaurant. Marco was already there, seated at a table in the window. He didn't see her straight away; he was too busy checking his wristwatch and looking more than a little irritated. She recalled Lando's warning about his hot Mediterranean temper.

She swallowed anxiously, hoping there wouldn't be any sort of scene. Luckily there weren't many other diners yet, so that was something. She hurried over to him.

'Marco, I'm so sorry.'

He glanced up, his expression instantaneously one of smiling pleasure. Becca relaxed. She'd been worrying about nothing.

'Becca, so good to see you again.' He got to his feet and, leaning towards her, dropped a kiss onto her cheek, just like the first time they'd met. However, this time his lips lingered, catapulting Becca's heart into overdrive. She could get to like this — and him. She smiled warmly back at him.

He walked around the table and pulled out her chair. 'Please, sit. I ordered a bottle of Pinot Grigio. I hope that's okay.'

Becca would actually have preferred red wine, but all she said was 'Wonderful' as she settled herself into her chair, preparing to enjoy the evening.

The waiter appeared with their wine. 'You can leave it, Luigi; I'll pour,' Marco told him, his gaze not leaving Becca. 'You look lovely again.'

She'd had her doubts about the dress she was wearing — was it too tight? Too low-cut? The wrong shade of green? But Marco's expression now told her it was exactly right. Usually she made every effort to disguise her curves, but this evening she'd decided to be brave. She'd purchased it six months ago, persuaded against her better judgement by the sales assistant that it suited her perfectly. 'It accentuates your lovely eyes,' she'd assured Becca. Even so, until this evening, she hadn't plucked up the courage to actually put it on. Now, seeing the admiration in Marco's eyes, she was glad she'd done so.

'The colour brings out your beautiful eyes.'

'Thank you,' she murmured, aware of the tide of warmth stealing up her face.

Another waiter handed them menus, and Becca gratefully hid behind hers as she concentrated on selecting her food.

Once again, the evening passed easily and enjoyably as Becca relaxed with her companion's engaging brand of humour. He proved to have an inexhaustible supply of amusing anecdotes, mainly tales about the things that happened while people were buying their cars. Becca, in turn, told him about some of the comical incidents that took place while she was visiting her grandmother.

'Where is she?' he asked.

'Birchfield Care Home, not far from here, actually. A couple of miles up the road. It makes it very easy to visit.'

'You're obviously close to her. Is she your maternal grandmother?'

'No, she's my father's mother. It almost destroyed her when he was killed.'

He stretched out his hand and covered one of hers. She'd already told him how her parents had died. 'But she must have found much consolation in having you with her.'

'She did, just as I found consolation in her. But as I said, she's never really got over it.' In fact, she often wondered whether the tragedy had in some way contributed to her mental decline some years later.

'You must take me with you to see her sometime.'

She regarded him in astonishment. 'You'd come with me? How kind.'

'Not really.' He squeezed her fingers. 'I'm becoming very fond of you, Becca.'

By the time they left the restaurant, Becca was convinced they could develop their relationship into something deeper. He was a kind man. Lando was wrong. She'd seen no evidence of a temper; none at all.

Marco walked her to her car, his fingers entwined with hers. When he finally helped her into the driving seat, he asked almost hesitantly, 'Can I see you again?'

She beamed up at him. 'I'd like that.'

'Good.' He leant in and kissed her, on her lips this time. Becca responded warmly. 'I'll ring you,' he murmured against her lips.

'Please,' she agreed.

She drove home feeling the happiest

she'd felt in a long time. She had a good feeling about Marco, but then her heart sank as she recalled her date on Monday with her third and final choice, Andy Gilmour. They'd arranged to meet at the Green Frog rather than the White Hart. She'd reasoned that being seen with too many different men in such rapid succession might give people the wrong idea about her. And the White Hart was the favourite pub for locals. She was tempted not to go, but for the second time, she couldn't bring herself to do that, so instead she resolved to keep the meeting brief. She'd make it clear she wasn't interested in any sort of prolonged relationship.

Which, as it turned out, didn't prove at all difficult. In complete contrast to how he'd appeared during the speed dating — moderately interesting, if a bit on the serious side — he turned out to be the most boring individual she'd ever had the misfortune to meet. From the second he sat down, he talked nonstop about himself. About his life, his job, his extensive — according to him — circle of friends. His car, of which he was inordinately proud. And much, much more. He barely allowed her the opportunity to say anything at all. So, not unexpectedly, after an hour of this, she found it increasingly difficult to control her yawns.

'Am I boring you?' he pointedly asked her.

'No, no,' she weakly protested. 'Not at all.'

But he took the hint, because the next thing he said was, 'Well, come on then, tell me about yourself. Do you still live with your family, or have you got a place of your own?' Judging by his tone of voice, it was clear he expected to be told no, she didn't.

Which guaranteed she relished saying, 'I have a place of my own.' She'd been astonished to learn that he still lived with his parents at the age of thirty-eight.

'You have?' He didn't make any

attempt to hide his disbelief. 'What? A bedsit?' His tone was patronising.

She was again extremely pleased to be able to say, 'No. A cottage. It needs a bit of work done on it, but . . . '

He sneered. 'Got it cheap, did you?'

The snide comment grated on her. 'Relatively,' she snapped.

'No family, then?'

'My grandmother.'

'Does she live with you? Maybe she helped you buy it?'

'No, I managed that all by myself.' She had no intention of telling him that without her inheritance from her parents, she couldn't possibly have afforded it. 'She's in Birchfield Care Home.'

'So what do you do, job wise? It must be something good. Someone's secretary, perhaps?' Again, his mouth twisted in a sneer.

Becca tightened her lips — a sure sign, if he did but know it, that she was becoming very irritated indeed. 'No. I have a beauty salon.'

'Do you?' He regarded her with deep scepticism.

She bluntly riposted, 'I do. A very successful one.' Which wasn't totally true. She and Lizzie struggled a lot of the time to make ends meet — well, if she was honest, it was most of the time — but she wasn't about to admit that to this objectionable man. Although things had begun to improve of late as they'd gradually built up their customer base. So much so, that some days both she and Lizzie were run off their feet. Sadly, it was only now and then, and any increase in their rent would almost certainly leave them struggling again.

As this was how the evening continued, it wasn't long before Becca grew weary of increasingly personal and snidely posed questions, and decided to call it quits. She'd spent more than enough time with him, listening to his patronising remarks. 'Well, it's been nice, but I really do have to go. I promised I'd look in on Gran and say good night.'

'At this time?' He made a point of checking his watch, which again infuriated Becca. It was nine o'clock.

'She'll still be up.' She wouldn't be, but Andy wasn't to know. And in any case, she had no intention of visiting. The truth was, if she had to spend another second in this man's company, she'd be pulling her hair out — or even worse, his hair. What a difference to how she'd felt about Marco.

'Well, we must meet again soon,' he went on, sublimely unaware of her urgent desire to get away from him. 'I feel we'd make a real team. The perfect couple, don't you think? Almost a match made in heaven?'

She looked at him, aghast. He couldn't really believe that, could he? Yet he did look very pleased with himself. Had he no inkling of how bored and irritated she'd been by him? How self-absorbed and deluded could a person be? 'Well, I'm pretty busy over the next few weeks.'

'Surely you can find time to see me?'

He did seem genuinely surprised by her comment. Hurt, even.

'I can't, I'm afraid. Not at the moment. What with Gran and my business, I don't have any spare time.' She shrugged helplessly, hoping he'd be convinced and wouldn't press her. There were only so many excuses she could come up with; credible ones, at least. 'I'm sorry.'

'Well, I'm sorry as well.' His expression was an extremely disgruntled one, if not resentful, as he yanked his jacket from the back of the chair and put it on. 'I just hope you don't regret it, because I'm rather busy too. And a missed opportunity is a lost opportunity.' His look then was a sneering one, obviously intended to make her aware of the mistake she was making. All it did, however, was ramp up her desire to get away from him, and hope she'd never have to see him again. Which she was sure was the last thing he intended.

Conceited jackass, she concluded. 'Okay, so I'll say goodnight then.' And before he could say or do anything more to prevent her leaving, she began to make her way to the door.

But it wasn't to be. Before she'd taken no more than a couple of paces, who should walk in with another man but Lando. He saw her at once, and she was forced to watch as his glance slid sideways to Andy. It must be perfectly obvious who she'd been with. She watched as his brow went up; he was visibly surprised at the sight of her with another man. However, that didn't stop him murmuring an aside to his companion before heading her way. The other man carried on to the bar, obviously primed to get their drinks in.

Becca's breath snagged in her throat at the manner in which he was regarding her; the way his gaze didn't leave her. Lord knew what he was thinking, having seen her with two different men in such a short time. Thank God he hadn't spotted her with Gary as well.

She wasn't left in ignorance of his

thoughts for long, however, because as he neared her, he said, 'What a surprise. Won't you introduce me?'

'Um — oh,' she stuttered.

Before she could utter more than that, Andy leapt in between them, holding out a hand. 'Andy Gilmour. So good to meet you, Wheatley. Your reputation precedes you. I've read all about you and your huge success in the *Financial Times*. Great photo, too. I was hoping I'd get to meet you, as we're both local men.' He gave a sickeningly ingratiating smile as he reached for and energetically shook Lando's hand.

Lando was not best pleased, that was very evident by his cool expression and equally cool 'Good evening.' After which, he firmly tugged his hand away, glancing back once more at Becca as he did so.

'My word, you do get around, don't you?' he murmured. 'Does Marco know about this tête-à-tête?'

Becca drew a deep breath. What was it with these men, that they seemed to assume they had a perfect right to dictate what she should and shouldn't do? She could meet who she damn well liked. Not surprisingly, her response was a predictably irritable one. 'I've no idea. I'm not answerable to Marco, or anyone else for that matter.'

'That's the whole purpose of a speed-dating evening, old man,' Andy put in to Becca's anguished dismay. 'You set up several dates and see which one you like best.' He gave a superior smile. 'You should try it sometime.'

'Thanks, but I'll pass on that one,' Lando snapped, his look one of total contempt at the other man. He then swept his gaze back to Becca, who was mortified to see the glint of mirth and — was that scorn contained within it? 'I wouldn't have thought you'd need to resort to that,' he softly murmured. 'But then it takes all sorts, I suppose.'

'Hey,' said Andy, thoroughly miffed by now, 'I object to your attitude, old man.'

Lando swung to him. 'I'm not your

old man. And, please, don't let us stop you from leaving.'

Andy, with a disgusted snort and another deeply resentful look at Becca, proceeded to stalk from the room. 'You'll be sorry.' He threw the words over his shoulder as he went.

Becca muttered, 'No, I won't be.' But she was also indignant at Lando's attitude. And she swung to him. 'It's none of your business what I do and who I see. But if you want the truth, it's a fun way to pass an evening. And that's all.'

'Fun? With that pretentious individual? But if it's fun you want, well . . . '

'If you're offering your services, please don't.'

Anger blazed at her then. 'Do you realise how dangerous what you're doing is? Meeting God knows who on your own?'

'I'm not on my own.' She made a point of glancing around the room. 'I'm in an almost-full pub.'

'You can't be interested in him.'

'I'm not. In fact, I've never had such a boring evening.'

'So,' he drawled, 'not altogether a success then? This speed-dating game?'

'Not on this occasion, no.' She couldn't mistake his satisfaction at her words. Odious man.

'Where are you off to now? To meet another candidate for a future relationship?'

'No. I'm heading back to my car and then home.'

'Where are you parked? I'll walk you.'

Surprised by his offer, she regarded him doubtfully. He was wearing a strange expression now. The satisfaction had vanished, and what replaced it looked remarkably like concern.

'There's no need. My car's only a couple of minutes' walk along the road.' It wasn't, however. It was at least a five-minute walk away; and what was more, it was down an unlit side road, the only space she'd been able to find.

'I'll see you back anyway. Who's to say that nutter isn't out there some-where, waiting for you?'

'He might be a bore, but he's not a nutter.'

'Sure of that, are you?'

She wasn't, but she wasn't about to say so. It would only prove him right in a convoluted sort of way. Instead, she sought refuge in silence.

Lando turned then and indicated to his companion, who was patiently waiting at the bar, that he'd be gone for a few minutes. It still rankled that he'd given her no option but to accept his offer. However, she did grudgingly concede that he had a point. She wasn't sure that Andy wouldn't be out there somewhere, waiting. He hadn't seemed to accept her refusal to see him again. Probably thought she was simply playing hard to get. It was the sort of conceit he would indulge in. In fact, she wouldn't be surprised if he rang or emailed her, hoping to persuade her to meet him again. A minuscule shiver went through her. She really hadn't liked him, or his attitude to her right at the end. He'd exhibited a worrying amount of hostility towards her, and definitely hadn't liked being turned down.

Lando shepherded her out of the pub, one hand on the back of her waist. 'Which way?' he asked.

She pointed left. 'Down here and then left again.'

'Left again?' he echoed. 'Isn't that an unlit side road? Whatever made you park there?'

'The fact that there were no other spaces, maybe?'

He didn't respond to that sarcastic gibe, other than to raise an eyebrow at her. 'You do seem to court danger, don't you?'

'Not deliberately, no.'

'Not even with that idiot at your side?'

'If you mean Andy — '

'That's exactly who I mean. I wouldn't trust him further than I could push him. Whatever made you agree to meet him?'

'He seemed perfectly nice at the . . . ' She faltered.

'Speed-dating evening?' he sarcastically finished for her.

Stung by this, she waspishly asked, 'Oh, so I'm safer with you, am I?'

'Considerably,' was his irritatingly smug response.

She didn't know what madness induced her to ask the next question, but ask it she did. 'Can I take it from that that you've recovered from your attraction to me?'

They'd reached her Polo by this time, and she stopped walking.

'This yours, is it?'

'It is.'

Lando turned his head and proceeded to examine her from beneath heavy lids. 'And in answer to your question, no, I haven't. Not by a long way.'

He was standing close to her; too close. What was more, he had her trapped between him and her car. Panic surged, swamping her. How did she know she could trust him any more than she could have trusted Andy? Her breathing quickened at the way his eyes were glittering at her through the darkness. And it was very dark here. There wasn't even a moon to beam its light down on them; clouds completely obscured it. An owl hooted from a nearby tree. Her unease deepened. He'd been very keen to walk with her. Too keen?

Desperately trying to give the impression of composure she was a million miles away from feeling, she tentatively asked, 'What-what does that mean?' Good grief, what a stupid question. What the hell did she think he meant?

She wasn't left wondering long, however, because he immediately murmured, the words low and throaty, 'It means that I desperately want to kiss you. How do you feel about that?'

5

'I — I don't know,' was all she managed to say.

As if heartened by her feeble response, he inched closer until their bodies were touching. The scent of his aftershave filled her nostrils. She breathed it in, and her senses instantly careered into a spin. The sheer masculinity of him overwhelmed her, thereby dispatching any lingering remnants of fear.

'Shall we find out then?' His words were low, throaty, seductive.

Becca's heartbeat thundered as her pulse rate accelerated. So intense was the effect he was having on her that words were beyond her.

Taking her silence for consent, Lando didn't hesitate. He brought one hand forward and cupped her chin, gently tilting her head backwards so that she was looking directly up at him. His gaze seared into her as it roamed lazily over her, from her wide eyes down to her parted lips. There it lingered. Her breath began to erupt in small gasps. She watched as he smiled, right before he lowered his head and captured her lips with his. She heard a soft groan and didn't know if it came from her or him. In another second, she didn't care which of them it was. His mouth was grinding almost brutally over hers, forcing her lips apart, allowing his tongue to slide inside and tangle with hers. He wrapped both arms about her then. Her breasts were pressed almost painfully against his chest. He moved a hand down to rest on her hips, moving her even closer, allowing her to feel every powerful line of him, before he slid a thigh between hers. It was a supremely sexual gesture, and one that made Becca's insides flame as passion engulfed her.

She'd never been kissed quite like this before. What was he doing to her?

And that was all it took. The words screamed inside her head: what the hell was she doing, allowing this accomplished womaniser to make love to her? Had she got no pride? She was almost certainly just one among many. Using both hands, she pushed him away.

'What are you doing?' she cried.

For a second, he just looked at her, almost bemusedly. 'You mean you don't know? I was kissing you. Where have you been all your life?'

'Yes, I know you were kissing me,' she snapped. 'But why?'

'Why?' Again he looked bemused. 'Because I wanted to, and you certainly didn't make any attempt to stop me. Therefore, naturally I assumed *you* wanted me to.'

'Well, I didn't,' she curtly told him. 'You assured me I'd be safe with you, but the truth is you're no different to any other man. The first opportunity you get, you're all over a woman, and I mean literally all over. It felt as if you'd got more arms than an octopus.'

He took another couple of steps back from her. 'Well, you certainly fooled me. You acted as if you wanted me to make love to you.'

'I did not,' she gasped.

'Becca.' His voice had softened. 'Look at me — please.'

As much as she wanted to take to her heels and run, she did look at him. His eyes had warmed again. Minute gold flecks gleamed at her.

'I'm sorry if I assumed too much.'

'You did. I'm not that easily available. And if that's the way I appeared, then I'm sorry too.'

Something flickered then in his eye, but as his lids quickly lowered, she didn't have time to work out what it was.

'Apology accepted. Now that's sorted out, I'll say goodnight and leave you.' He paused, still staring at her. 'You'd better unlock your car and get inside. The road's too dark to leave you alone.'

A flood of shame swamped Becca then. Despite her furious rejection of him, he still cared what happened to her. Could she have misjudged him? She stared up at him, searching for some sign that she had. But she could see nothing. His expression was impassive; every indication of passion, of desire, had vanished. And she had been told of his dubious reputation with women. Something had fuelled that rumour.

Still, she couldn't leave things there. 'Lando,' she said.

'What?'

'Thank you.'

He didn't speak. He simply raised an eyebrow.

'F-for seeing me back here. And again, I'm sorry.'

'As I am for so badly misjudging the situation. I'm not usually that insensitive.' His tone was a dry one.

Becca turned away without responding and opened her car door. She got in, fastened her seat belt, started the engine and drove away. Lando watched her go, his expression a thoughtful one as he finally turned and made his way back to the restaurant.

Neither of them had noticed the car passing by while they'd been locked in their embrace. But the driver had certainly noticed them and, what was more, even given the lack of street lighting, had recognised Becca. It was pure chance that he'd taken that route home, otherwise he'd never have known what had happened. His eyes had glinted with fury. She was his, and she'd have to be taught that. Taught to see him as the one who would rescue her from a life of misery with the wrong man; the only one who could.

* * *

As for Becca, she barely slept that night as she replayed, over and over, the passionate lovemaking she and Lando had shared. He'd been fully aroused, she'd been only too aware of that. He hadn't tried to hide it, pressing her close to him as he had. In fact, it had been as if he had wanted her to know. She groaned. She should never have succumbed to his kisses. She barely knew him, for God's sake.

By the time morning came, she'd only had a couple of hours of sleep at best, with the result that she turned up at the salon with shadowed eyes and a face drained of colour.

'Good Lord,' Lizzie cried, 'what's wrong with you? Can I assume your date with number three didn't go well? What was this one called?'

'Andy.'

'That's the one. So what happened? I want all the gory details.'

'Believe me, they'd bore you rigid.' They wouldn't, of course. Lizzie liked nothing better than a good old gossip.

'Does that mean Andy didn't live up to expectations?'

'It certainly does. A more boring man I've yet to meet. He spent the better part of the evening droning on about himself ad nauseam. When he did ask about me, my every response was met with sarcasm and resentment. He clearly doesn't like to hear about a woman managing for herself without a man at her side, guiding her, instructing her. Egotistical pig.'

'Wow! He really did get on your wrong side.'

'He did.'

Lizzie eyed her then. 'You know, you could do worse than give Sam another chance.'

'It's no good, Lizzie. I don't have the right sorts of feelings for Sam. He deserves someone better, and hopefully he's found her.'

* * *

But things seemed set to take a turn for the better that evening. Marco rang.

'Hi, Marco,' she greeted him. 'How are you?'

'I'm fine.'

He didn't sound it, however. He

sounded irritated. 'What's wrong?'

'I rang you last evening but you must have been out.'

'I was, yes.'

'Where?'

'Um — well, I met the third date from the speed-dating event.'

'I see.'

The silence then seemed to go on and on, compelling her to ask, 'Marco? Are you still there?'

'Yes. The thing is, I didn't expect you to meet anyone else, not after the way we clicked.'

Becca was aware of a sense of dismay. She hadn't considered Marco viewing her date with such displeasure. In fact, she'd fully expected that he too would have had some other meetings set up. That had been the whole point of the evening, after all.

'I did consider cancelling, but it seemed rude, so I decided to go ahead with it. Believe me,' she said with a chuckle, 'I won't be repeating the experience.'

This remark was once again met with an uncomfortable silence.

'Marco?'

'I'm here. Does that mean you'll only be seeing me?'

'Quite possibly.' She smiled to herself. He was jealous. How sweet.

'Don't,' he curtly bade her.

'Marco.' She couldn't conceal her dismay. She wasn't accustomed to being ordered around by anyone, much less a man she'd only just met. This wasn't how things were meant to go.

'Please, don't tease me. I'm serious. I don't like to think of you seeing other men.'

'I-I didn't mean to tease.' She had, though, she freely admitted.

'Then why did you?'

'I don't know. I'm sorry.'

'Okay.'

His acceptance of her apology sounded grudging. She wished she could see his face, his expression. A feeling of unease crept through her. The majority of men would have taken her remark in the spirit it was meant, jokingly. Not this one, clearly. Damn. The last thing she needed was a possessive man. Especially one she'd only met a couple of times.

'I was ringing to see if you wanted to meet me this evening.' His tone remained cool.

Again, she felt a tad uneasy. 'Oh, Marco — I'm afraid I'm totally knackered. I've had a crazy day, and all I want is a hot bath and bed. How about tomorrow?' The truth was, she couldn't face spending an evening treading on eggshells, picking her way round an oversensitive man. Last night had been bad enough, being literally bored almost to death. In fact, death would have been the preferable option. And then in the wake of that, the argument with Lando ... No, she couldn't face another potentially difficult evening.

'Okay, if that's what you wish.'

He still sounded cool, formal. The ease she'd felt on their previous meetings vanished. Would it return?

'There's a new wine bar opened in Green Street,' he went on. 'I thought we could try it. Or have you already been there with someone else?' He still sounded waspish.

Becca gave a soft sigh. Why were men so difficult? So demanding? This was how it had ended with Sam. He'd wanted to know everything she'd been doing between their meetings. In the end, it became insufferable, and had been the main reason for finishing with him.

However, now she managed to inject a degree of enthusiasm into her tone. 'Sounds great. What time?'

'Eight?'

'Okay. See you there.'

She put the phone down, her expression troubled. That hadn't gone at all well. Marco had revealed a previously unexpected side to himself. A disturbingly possessive side. What on earth would he say if he found out about Lando kissing her? In fact, precisely what was she getting herself into here?

⋆ ⋆ ⋆

The following evening provided an answer of sorts. Marco was totally different to how he'd been on their previous meetings. He keenly quizzed her, demanding to know what she'd been doing that day, almost minute by minute. Asking if she had indeed spent the previous evening at home, alone. Once again, she wondered if she was doing the right thing, getting involved with a man who clearly wanted to dominate. She'd always been independent, strong-willed, even as a girl. And with her parents' premature deaths, that side of her character had developed unhindered. The mere idea of having to bow to someone else's wishes and demands wasn't a welcome one. But it was early days with Marco. He was evidently a bit insecure. He needed to trust that she wouldn't mess him around. She wondered if some woman had hurt him at some time; been unfaithful, maybe.

Determined to find out, she asked, 'Tell me about yourself, as a boy, a teenager. What about your parents, for example? You haven't mentioned them.'

His mouth tightened as his eyes darkened. 'My mother ran off when I was thirteen. Left my father and me for another man. I haven't seen her since.'

'Not at all?' Becca was horrified, but it could explain his insecurity, his distrust of her.

He shrugged. 'The odd birthday card, that's all. Then my father died eighteen months later. Of a broken heart, people said.'

'Marco . . . ' She stretched out a hand to him. ' . . . I'm so sorry.'

'Oh, no need to be. I'm long over it. I'm a man now, no longer a boy. I have a good life.'

'So what did you do after your father died? Did you have other family?'

'Yes, an aunt who took me in until I

finished my education. I came to the UK not long after.'

It was all sounding remarkably similar to her life, except that both her parents had died. No wonder he was insecure and unable to trust anyone. His mother, the woman who should have loved and cared for him above all else, had abandoned him.

'And girlfriends? Friends?'

'Several, of both sexes. I've had no serious relationships, however. Not until now, that is.' He squeezed her fingers, his eyes blazing with emotion. 'You're different, Becca. I think — no, I know — I love you.'

Becca's heart shifted in her breast — but not in joy, more in apprehension; a deep misgiving, in fact. It was far too soon for such a declaration.

'Uh — Marco, let's take things slowly, eh?'

He stared at her. 'Why? Can't you see how right we are together? We're meant for each other. It is Fate,' he solemnly pronounced.

Oh, good grief. Another man assuming too much. This was moving way too fast. Somehow she had to cool things without hurting him. That was the last thing she wanted to do after what he'd just told her. But how?

She began, 'Marco, give it time. We barely know each other.'

'I know you,' he indignantly told her. 'I know I want you and that I can make you want me.'

'No, you don't know that, any more than I know it.'

'How can you say that? We've talked intimately. I've told you things I've never told anyone else. About my parents.'

Becca didn't know what to say. She stared at him.

'You've told me about yourself,' he went on.

'But that isn't enough to embark upon a serious relationship. It takes more than the sharing of a few secrets.'

'No, you're wrong.' He let go of her hand. 'Have you never heard of love at first sight? Or am I wasting my time?' His eyes flashed with anger. 'I believed, really believed, that we had a chance of something good, real; something lasting. Obviously I was wrong.' He got to his feet. 'I'd better leave.'

Becca, too, struggled to her feet. 'Marco — please. I don't want it to end like this. I enjoy your company, I do, but I need time.'

'And you'll have it, Becca. I'll leave you alone to consider things. And when — no, if — you decide you want to continue this, then contact me.' He lifted his wine glass and drained it of the last drops before replacing it on the table. Then, without another word, he strode from the bar.

Helplessly, Becca watched him go. But despite her original hope that he could be the one, she felt an unexpected sense of relief. She wasn't ready for something as intense as Marco seemed to want. And now, with the evidence of his possessive nature, she acknowledged that he wasn't the one for her. Lando had been right about him, much as she hated admitting it.

Realising she'd become the focus of everyone's attention, she sat down again. She then finished her drink before slipping on her jacket, paying the bill, and finally, with a face that was hot with embarrassment, left.

What a disaster. And it had all happened so fast. She checked her watch and saw that it was only eight forty-five. She'd give Lizzie a ring and see if she fancied a drink. Not at the wine bar; she couldn't face all the curious glances again. But the White Hart was usually reasonably quiet midweek.

Lizzie answered almost at once. 'Hi, Becca. What's up? I thought you were seeing Marco this evening.'

'I was.'

'And?'

'It's over.'

'Wow! That was quick, even for you. What happened?'

'Could we meet at the White Hart?

I'll tell you then.'

'Well, we could, but Sam's here with me. He was at a loose end, so we've had dinner together.' Becca heard the low murmur of voices, then Lizzie added, 'Would you mind if he came too? He'd love to see you, catch up.' Lizzie's tone was one of uncertainty.

'Okay, but . . . ' She lowered her voice. ' . . . he does realise there's no chance of him and me — ?'

'Yeah, yeah. Don't worry about that. He's cool.'

'Okay, see you both in fifteen minutes or so.'

Lizzie's one-bedroom flat was only five minutes by car from the town centre. 'Make it twenty,' she said. 'I need to clear up here and then change. Get me a large glass of Merlot and a pint for Sam. Put it on a tab and we'll settle up at the end of the evening.'

'Okay. See you then.'

Becca carried on along the high street to the White Hart. It was at the opposite end to the wine bar. She'd left her car in a small central car park so it would be convenient for both venues. She was halfway there when a horn sounded right behind her. Her heart leapt. Had Marco had second thoughts? But when she swivelled, it was to see not Marco, but Lando, sitting in a silver Jaguar and pulling into the kerbside.

6

Lando slid the passenger window down and asked, 'Can I give you a lift somewhere?'

'There's no need, thank you. I'm only headed for the White Hart with a friend. My partner in the salon, Lizzie.' Why the hell had she told him that? It was none of his business. Though as they were renting the salon from him, maybe it was.

'I didn't realise you had a partner. But that will be perfect. Would you mind if I joined you both? I have some news.'

'News?'

'Yes, on the work I was talking about doing on the front of the shops.'

'I see.'

What now? Had he got his planning permission? He looked pretty pleased with himself, so probably. Her heart sank at the prospect that Lizzie would be present to hear that. God knew how she'd react.

As if she hadn't had enough to put up with already this evening, now she had to face the likelihood of a row between her partner and their landlord. She was sorely tempted to stand them all up and just go home. She sighed. She couldn't do that. Knowing her friend's outspokenness, the meeting could very well end with their tenancy being cut short and their eviction from the salon. If she was there, she could at least try to mediate, make sure that didn't happen.

'Right. I'll go and park then and see you there.' And he drove off without another word. Deliberately? To keep her guessing? She wouldn't put it past him. As the head of a large company, well, group of companies, he'd be only too accustomed to controlling both people and events.

She trudged onwards, feeling for all the world as if she were approaching her doom. She'd only just found a table for four, having got the drinks from the bar, when Lando strode in. His swift glance round located her and he headed her way via the bar where he ordered his own drink. However, as he approached her she saw that he was holding a bottle of red wine. He chose the seat immediately opposite her. Oh God. Now there'd be no escaping his scrutiny. He'd be able to see her every expression.

'I thought this would be easier, and I know you drink red.'

'Thank you, but as you can see — ' She indicated the three glasses on the table. ' — I've already got the drinks in.' If he thought he could buy her off with a few glasses of wine, he could think again.

'Well, I'm sure you'll want more than one,' he said, filling his own glass as he did so. He then raised it and said, 'Cheers,' before adding, 'Your partner not here yet?'

'Here she is.' She'd spotted Lizzie

and Sam walking in. Lando turned to look in the direction she'd indicated.

'Who's the man? Your partner's date or yours?'

'He's an old friend, and he's Lizzie's brother. But yes,' she tersely added in response to the gleam that lit his eye, 'we did go out together at one time.' *So stick that in your pipe.*

'He doesn't look your type.'

Becca was all set to demand what he thought her type was when Lizzie said, 'Hi.' Her glance went instantly to Lando, suspicion and speculation plastered all over her face.

Lando stood up and held out a hand. 'Lando Wheatley. I hope you don't mind me joining you all.'

'I'm Lizzie and this is my brother, Sam. And no, I don't mind you joining us. In fact, you're just the person I wanted to speak to. You've saved me the bother of tracking you down.' She gave him the sort of smile that indicated trouble.

Oh no, Becca glumly reflected, she

was intending to tackle him about his plans. 'Urn — Lizzie,' she cut in, 'Lando has some news for us, apparently. Her expression signalled to wait and hear what he had to say before charging in, all guns blazing.

Lizzie took the hint and plumped herself down into the chair right next to Lando. Becca's heart fell and dropped even further when Sam immediately settled himself next to her. He leant over and kissed her on the cheek. 'This is an unexpected treat, Bex. How long's it been?'

Becca eyed him. 'Uh, the week before last, wasn't it? In the White Hart? You were with, uh — Mel, was it? She looked nice.'

'Oh, yeah.' He snorted with laughter. 'I'd forgotten about that.' He slid an arm around her shoulders and pulled her nearer, saying, 'Bex and I are old friends.'

Becca dared a glance at Lando and saw what could only be described as vexation in the slaty eyes as his glance went first of all to Sam, and then swept sideways to her. Her heartbeat quickened, as did her breathing. His expression instantly changed to one of quiet satisfaction. She couldn't believe it. He'd detected her response to him. Did the wretched man have some sort of inbuilt radar?

'Okay,' Lizzie broke in impatiently, 'let's hear this news.'

Lando took his time in turning his glance to her. 'The planning permission has been granted for the work on the shops to begin.'

Lizzie looked momentarily stunned. However, she made a superfast recovery to say, 'Wow! That was quick. You must have a great deal of influence with someone.'

Becca anxiously awaited the sort of putdown she knew Lando was capable of. To her astonishment, though, all he said was, 'It wasn't down to any sort of influence on my part, I can assure you of that. The fact is, I applied for it right after I bought the shops. But I agree, it's been quick. Mainly because the planning people — and the council — are keen to spruce up the town in order to encourage more shoppers in from the surrounding area.'

Lizzie rolled her eyes disparagingly before snapping, 'How very convenient for you. So how much are the rents to go up? And, more importantly, when's the work going to begin? Because it'll prove very disruptive for us all'

Becca briefly closed her eyes as dismay took over. *Here we go*, she reflected. *Let the battle begin.* She found herself again hoping they'd still have a salon by the end of the evening.

But she was surprised once more when all Lando said was, 'Hopefully not. We'll make every effort to minimise that. In any case, work won't start until the spring, so you'll have plenty of time to prepare yourselves.'

'Oh, how kind,' Lizzie sarcastically cooed, steadfastly ignoring Becca's glance, a glance that pleaded, *Don't overdo it-please.*

'No,' Lando said, ignoring the sarcasm, 'not kind, just plain old common sense. Winter isn't really suitable for carrying out exterior renovation work. The weather's far too unreliable. Anyway, we have several other projects to complete first.'

'Really? What are those?' This time it was Becca doing the asking.

Lando met her gaze across the table. 'Well, for starters, there's the new housing estate on the old carpet factory site.'

'Oh, that's you, is it?'

He nodded.

'You faced a bit of a protest there too, didn't you?'

'A little, but people soon realised the benefit it would be to the town. Half of the homes are going to be starter homes, which I believe are in very short supply in these parts.' His expression now was a challenging one.

However, since no one could reasonably argue against that — it was something local people had been grumbling about for years — Becca said nothing.

Lizzie seemed grimly determined to bring the conversation back to a much more important topic. 'You haven't actually said — how much will our rents go up?'

'I'm not sure they will. If we can manage to stay inside budget, it shouldn't be necessary. But if it is, it won't be a large rise. The increased custom that will almost certainly come your way should more than compensate for it.'

'You can't be sure we'll get more customers, though, can you? This is all very easy for you to say.'

'Yes, I learned to speak at a very early age.'

Becca watched as Lizzie struggled to suppress a grin, deciding that maybe it was time to change the subject. 'How are your own renovations coming on?' she asked.

'Barely started, I'm afraid to say. I'm undecided about how to go about it. I've never faced such a challenge before.'

'Sounds like you need professional advice and help.'

He cocked his head at her. 'I'm still hoping you'll come and have a look.'

Becca sensed Lizzie's sudden surge of curiosity. She also felt Sam stiffening at her side. He abruptly removed his arm from her shoulders and said, 'I didn't realise you two knew each other so well.'

'Oh, we don't,' Becca hastened to assure him. 'Our encounters have been very brief.'

'Huh.' Sam snorted disparagingly. 'Sounds like the title of a bloody film.'

'I'm hoping that situation will soon change,' Lando murmured.

Sam then blurted, 'And does Bex feel the same way?'

'Bex,' Lando repeated, 'that's an unusual abbreviation for Rebecca.'

'It's what I've always called her.' He squeezed Becca's hand as he stared straight into her eyes. 'You don't mind, do you?'

'Well, I prefer Becca if you want the

truth.' Which she'd pointed out several times during their dating days; he'd stubbornly disregarded her protests, and so she'd remained Bex. Another reason, in her view, to end the relationship. She simply hadn't been able to face spending the rest of her life being called Bex. It sounded like an indigestion tablet.

'It seems a shame to shorten a lovely name like Rebecca at all,' Lando said, lifting his glass to his lips while at the same time watching Becca across the rim.

Becca felt the beginnings of a blush. Dammit, why couldn't she break this ridiculously juvenile habit? It was unbecoming for a woman of twenty-seven. However, Lando clearly didn't feel the same way, because his mouth quivered with the beginnings of a smile as he continued to watch her. She glared at him, which, disappointingly, had no effect at all.

To make matters even worse, she felt Sam's arm slide across her shoulders again. 'Bex and I were an item for quite a while.' This remark was solely for Lando's benefit, Becca guessed. Which ensured that her irritation with both of them intensified. She was beginning to feel like a piece of meat, being argued over by two self-centred and arrogant men. She shifted impatiently, thereby removing herself from Sam's grasp. She then unobtrusively slid her chair to one side, ensuring she was out of his reach. He didn't notice.

Lando, however, did. 'Clearly you're not still an item.' The sarcasm of the final two words went unnoticed by Sam. 'I've never really understood that term. An item? How can two people be an item?' However, both Becca and Lizzie heard it. Becca fought to hide a smile, while Lizzie simply looked annoyed.

'An item as in a couple. One couple,' Sam irritably pointed out. He reached once more for Becca and, by dint of leaning sideways, managed to get hold of her arm. He tugged at it, trying to pull her closer.

Becca's feeling of being no more than a piece of meat grew. 'Sam, don't,' she spoke sharply, drawing Sam's hurt gaze to her.

'What's wrong, and why have you moved your chair?' He'd only just noticed.

'Because I don't want to be tugged and pulled around.'

'Oh, well — pardon me,' he muttered, after which he sought consolation in a large mouthful of beer.

Hoping to ease her own tension, Becca also took refuge in a generous mouthful of wine, and then another, swiftly followed by a third. All were mistakes. Mainly because she'd also drunk a large glassful with Marco. This whole evening was turning into a nightmare. She felt her head spin.

Taking pity on her, Lizzie changed the subject by impetuously and tactlessly asking her, 'Can I assume your date with Marco didn't go well, as it's over so early in the evening?'

Both men's gazes moved to her. She indulged in another gulp of her wine. Her head spun even more dizzily. She glowered at her almost empty glass, as if it the whole debacle was in some way the fault of the glass.

'Marco?' Sam was the first to exclaim. 'Who the hell's Marco?'

'Just someone I met.'

'He's an employee of mine,' Lando cut in. 'So what happened, Becca?'

'Nothing. Well, things just . . . didn't work out this evening for some reason. But . . . it's early days.' She struggled to come up with excuses. She didn't want to have to admit that Lando had been right — Marco did have a temper, as well as an extremely possessive streak. And she certainly didn't want to talk about it in front of Sam.

Fortunately, conversation took a more general turn after this, Lizzie in particular quizzing Lando about his life to date. She'd obviously decided to put her concerns over the rent rise to one side for the moment, much to Becca's relief. Lando didn't look as if he minded being questioned, and freely told her about his various business interests, mainly in the UK, but also in Europe. He owned a chain of car showrooms, as well as a string of hotels in the south of France and Spain. She also learned that Lizzie had been right about him buying ailing companies and bringing them back to profit before selling them on once more. All in the UK. And that was aside from his property development business. No wonder he'd made oodles of money, thus enabling him to buy Ashleigh House.

As for Sam, he didn't say very much at all, but what he did say was on the whole critical of Lando. Lando didn't look as if he'd taken offence, apart from a couple of occasions when Sam really did push things, driving Lando to respond with a chilling curtness. In the end, Sam lapsed into a sulky silence.

When the time came to leave, Lando quietly said, 'Becca, I suggest you leave your car wherever it is and pick it up in the morning. I'll run you home.'

'I'll take a taxi.'

Lizzie cut in, 'I'll take you. Lando's right, you shouldn't drive.' 'No, Lizzie, it's in the opposite direction for you. And you've had a drink too.'

'Yeah, but not as much as you have,' Lizzie drily retaliated.

Lando, however, took matters into his own hands and strode round to Becca's side. 'Come on. It's been decided. I'll take.'

'Hey, hey, Bex said no.' Sam leapt to his feet. 'If anyone takes her, I will.'

Lando again cut in, 'Do you have a car?'

'Well, no — but I can use Lizzie's.'

'Then how will Lizzie get home?' Lando argued. 'This is ridiculous. I have to more or less pass your cottage, Becca.'

'No, you don't,' Becca argued. However, she didn't want Sam driving her home. He'd want to come inside, judging by his proprietorial manner towards her throughout the evening, and then they'd doubtless end up rowing, with accusations being hurled back and forth — the last thing she wanted.

'The matter's settled.' Again, this was Lando speaking. 'I'm taking you.'

'All right,' Becca grudgingly relented.

'Good.' He turned to the other two. Sam was still scowling at the way things had turned out, and said, 'I'll say goodnight. It's been nice to meet you both.'

'It's been good to meet you too,' Lizzie agreed. 'Always handy to know your enemy. What is it they say? Keep your friends close and your enemies closer.'

Lando didn't respond to this other than to smile coolly and murmur, 'I'm sure we can work something out.'

Still, Lizzie couldn't resist adding, 'I certainly hope so, otherwise I predict a stormy period ahead.'

7

'She always has to have the last word,' Becca muttered as Lando steered her through the pub doorway.

'Well, she does have a point. It is always useful to know one's enemy. In fact, I make a habit of it.'

I'm sure you do, Becca reflected before asking, 'Where are you parked?' Her words were ever so slightly slurred. Whatever must he be thinking of her?

She slanted a look at him, but he showed no sign of censure, simply saying, 'Just up ahead. In front of the library.'

'That's good. I can't face a long walk.'

'I wouldn't imagine you could,' he drily agreed.

She turned her head and subjected him to a suspicious frown. He was still holding on to her. 'You can let go of me now, you know. I can walk on my own.'

'Sure about that, are you?'

'Of course.'

He let go. She instantly staggered sideways.

'Maybe not,' he murmured, reaching out for her again.

'You let go too suddenly. I-I wasn't prepared,' she snapped.

'Whatever. But, if you don't mind, I'll keep hold of you. Don't want you falling at my feet, do we?'

'Huh! As if,' she snorted.

'That unpleasant a prospect, is it?'

He sounded miffed. Becca slanted a glance at him. He met it with a level glance of his own, but refrained from passing any further comment.

'Here we are,' he told her a few seconds later. 'My car.' He opened the passenger door and helped her inside. He then leant across her and fastened the seat belt.

Becca's head began to whirl once more, and this time it wasn't due to her intoxication. The scent of his aftershave and the proximity of him was all it took. 'You smell good,' she breathed.

He turned his head and regarded her. His face was only an inch or so from hers, as was his mouth. 'Thank you.' From the quiver of his voice, it was evident he was trying very hard not to laugh. 'You don't smell too bad yourself.'

He straightened up, closed the door and strode around to the driver's side. Within seconds, he was starting the engine, and the car slid away from the kerb, purring softly as it did so.

'Nice car. Very comfortable.' Becca leant back into her seat and closed her eyes. She was so tired . . .

'Becca, wake up.'

'Wh-what? I wasn't asleep,' she indignantly told him.

'You always snore while awake, do you?'

'I don't snore.' She was horrified. Oh God. Was she dribbling too? Surreptitiously, she dabbed at her lips.

Of course he noticed. The corners of

his mouth quirked, betraying his amusement. The wretched man did have some sort of built-in radar; she was becoming increasingly convinced of that.

'Oh, don't worry. It was done in a very ladylike fashion.' This time he grinned broadly, making no attempt to disguise his mirth. She glowered at him. 'Anyway, we're back. Stay where you are. I'll come round and help you out.'

She didn't argue. Frankly, she hadn't got the energy. He helped her out onto the driveway and then guided her to the front door.

'Do you want to give me your key?'

'Yeah,' she muttered, undoing the catch of her handbag and rummaging around inside, before finally pulling out the key, only to promptly drop it.

Lando bent over and picked it up before opening the door. He then proceeded to steer her inside before asking, 'Where's the sitting room?'

'There.' She pointed to the door right ahead of them.

Once inside the room, he led her to the settee. She sat down before remembering her manners and asking, 'Oh — do you want a cup of coffee?'

'I think you do. If you point me in the direction of the kitchen, I'll make you one.'

Deciding it was easier by far to simply do as he asked, she said, 'Into the hall, and it's the door on the left.' She leant back into the settee cushions and again closed her eyes. It seemed the best thing to do. Mainly because the room had begun to spin disconcertingly around her. Seconds later — at least, that was the way it felt — Lando was back, carrying two cups of coffee. He placed them on the low table in front of the settee and took his seat alongside her.

Once again, the aroma of his aftershave filled her nostrils. She inhaled deeply; her head reeled. This was bad, she decided.

'Are you okay?' he asked.

'I will be.'

'Here.' He handed her one of the cups. 'Drink this. It should help steady you.'

She took it from him and slowly sipped at the hot liquid. Lando lifted his own cup and took a couple of mouthfuls, his gaze not leaving her.

Once Becca had drunk the entire contents of the cup, she set it back on its saucer. She was acutely aware of Lando still watching her and dredged up a shaky smile.

'Better?'

'A little.' She gazed back at him and felt a tremendous surge of emotion rise within her. He was so handsome, so kind. Why was he being so kind? She'd been beastly to him.

But then, and without knowing why, she leant towards him and pressed her mouth to his. She felt his start of surprise, but she couldn't stop herself. Desire swamped her, the desire to feel his arms around her, to feel his mouth ravaging hers again.

He didn't do anything for a long,

long moment, and then he was kissing her back. She parted her lips to him, and felt his arms go round her as he pulled her close. She groaned as he deepened the kiss. His arms tightened, pressing her against him. She slid her arms up his chest and around his neck. Her fingers strayed into his hair, the strands silky smooth against her finger-tips. But then, unexpectedly and way, way too soon, he was pushing her away.

She stared up at him, eyes wide with bewilderment, lips still parted. Oh no. She repulsed him. He didn't want her. She probably reeked of the wine she'd drunk. How embarrassing.

'Don't look at me like that.' His voice was rough, low.

'Wh-what's wrong?'

'Everything. You've had far too much to drink.'

'That doesn't matter.' She was right. She repelled him.

'To me it does. I don't make love to intoxicated women.'

'S-sorry, does my breath smell?' She

covered her mouth with her hand. She did reek of alcohol.

'No, it's not that. I make it a habit not to take advantage of a woman who's not in full control of her senses, that's all.'

She took her hand away and slumped back once more into the cushions. 'I'm not that drunk.'

'Maybe not, but I'm still not making love to you.' His words were harsh; inflexible.

She glared at him. 'You were keen enough the other night, and I'd had a drink then.'

He stared at her, his head to one side, his eyes narrowed to slits. 'And I'll still be keen when you've sobered up. Come to my house on Saturday evening — for dinner, that's all.' His smile told her that he'd read her thoughts; thoughts that had been all about him making love to her — properly. 'You can tell me what you think about it. Give me some ideas.'

'Okay. What time?'

He didn't bother hiding his smile, making Becca cringe with yet more embarrassment. She'd sounded too eager, shamelessly so.

'Eight o'clock-ish. We'll talk then, and you can tell me all about Marco.' His tone had hardened as he mentioned the other man's name. 'And you can tell me what he did that made you leave so early in the evening.'

'He's too possessive,' she muttered. 'Way too demanding. He wants me all to himself.'

'We-ell, that figures.' He eyed her. 'So you don't care for jealous men?'

'No.'

'I see. I'll have to watch myself then. Because I freely admit, I don't like sharing my women either. You're either with me or you're not,' he bluntly concluded.

'Oh.' She didn't know what to say to that.

'So I'll see you on Saturday, then?'

She nodded.

'I'll see myself out.'

'You're going?' She couldn't hide her dismay.

'I think I'd better. I only have so much self-control. Don't want to find myself behaving like an octopus again, do I?' he murmured provocatively.

She couldn't help but grin at him then. He was quoting her own words back at her. 'I see.'

'Do you?'

'Oh yes. Till Saturday.'

He leant towards her and dropped a light kiss onto her nose. Daringly, Becca moved her head so that his kiss ended up on her lips before she quickly drew back again. 'Bye,' she saucily added, thus eliciting a somewhat regretful look from him.

* * *

However, come the next morning, her emotions about going to Lando's house on Saturday suffered a dramatic turnaround. What the hell had possessed her to agree to such a thing? And why,

141

in heaven's name, had she kissed him? What had she been thinking? She *hadn't* been thinking, that was the problem. She'd been far too intoxicated. He'd been right about that.

She buried her face in both hands. More to the point was what he had thought. That she'd given him the come-on to make love to her? Was that what he planned for Saturday? God, she'd practically asked him for it. She climbed from bed, her most fervent wish being to die right there and then. Maybe she could cancel? Email him? No, that would be cowardly. And what would she say? He'd see straight through any excuse she might make. He was proving astonishingly perceptive, seemingly reading her thoughts almost before she had them.

Queen Bee wound herself around her ankles as she walked unsteadily into the kitchen, almost tripping her up as she meowed piteously.

'Okay, I'll feed you first.' She tore open a pouch of cat food and emptied it into the cat bowl. 'There you are.' She then set about making herself a cup of very strong coffee. That would soon put her right.

Three cupfuls later, she did feel marginally better. At least her head had stopped pounding. If only her fears about Saturday evening would also ease.

She began to get ready to go to work, resisting the impulse to ring Lizzie and say she couldn't make it. Lizzie would know instantly what was wrong. In any case, going to work would surely take her mind off Lando Wheatley.

Oh no, dammit — she'd left her car in town the evening before. She'd have to walk, which meant she'd probably be late, unless she left straight away. Oh well, the exercise should see off the remaining dregs of her hangover.

However, that hope clearly hadn't been fulfilled, because the minute she walked through the door into the salon — only five minutes late, fortunately — Lizzie took one look at her and said,

'Oh dear, not feeling quite the thing this morning?'

'You could say that. How much did I actually drink last night?'

'More than enough, obviously,' Lizzie drily remarked.

'I need a coffee before my first appointment.' She checked the wall clock. She had ten minutes to spare. 'Do you want one? Have you got time?'

'Yeah.' She followed Becca into the back room. 'How did you get on with the handsome Mr Wheatley?'

'Fine,' Becca muttered, concentrating on spooning the coffee into their mugs.

'Did he behave himself? Because methinks he's taken a fancy to you.'

'Don't be ridiculous.'

'Is that what I'm being?'

'Yes. He's way out of my league.'

'Handy, though. You can maybe influence him over the rent rises.'

'And how will I go about that?'

'Feminine wiles? You know.'

'No, Lizzie.'

Lizzie narrowed her gaze at her. 'Did

he try something last night?'

'No, but . . . ' She didn't know whether to tell Lizzie about going to his house or not.

'Go on, but — what?'

'He's invited me to his house on Saturday evening.'

'Wow! He mentioned that in the pub. I didn't think he was serious.' She eyed Becca. 'Are you going?'

'I thought I might. Purely on an advisory basis.'

Lizzie rolled her eyes and hooted with laughter. 'Yeah, right. Who are you trying to kid? You fancy him.'

Becca busied herself with stirring the coffee.

'Go on, admit it.'

'We-ell, maybe, but nothing will come of it. He's probably just toying with me.' She handed Lizzie her mug. 'Drink that and let's get to work.' And that was the end of that particular conversation, for the moment at least. Knowing Lizzie as well as she did, she'd eventually return to it, if only to persuade Becca to try and convince Lando he shouldn't raise the rent.

★　★　★

It was the following night, at eleven thirty exactly, that Becca's landline phone rang. It was a little unusual, because her friends invariably used the mobile number, and they wouldn't ring this late anyway. Fleetingly, she wondered if it could be Lando. Cancelling their date, maybe? Disappointment stabbed at her. Oh no. She couldn't be falling for him, could she? Could Lizzie be right?

She went into the hall and lifted the handset to her ear. 'Hello?' There was no response. 'Hello? Who is this?' Still no one replied. Instead, all she could hear was the sound of someone breathing before whoever it was ended the call. She replaced the handset only for it to ring again a couple of moments later. Exactly the same thing happened. Vexed now, she cut the call. It was a bit late for it to be one of those nuisance sales calls, surely? When it rang again for a third time, she ignored it. Whoever it was would soon get fed up. They did, eventually; it took six calls altogether.

However, it started her thinking. Nuisance calls weren't usually so persistent, which led her to wonder if that was all it had been. She'd heard of people who did this sort of thing just for the hell of it. It was how they got their kicks, scaring women late at night. She decided to call 1471, but the customary digital tones informed her that there was no number to return the call.

Eventually she went up to bed, deciding to put it down to someone mischievously passing the time. She'd be at Lando's the next evening and probably wouldn't be home till late. So if whoever it had been should decide to play the same games then, she wouldn't be around to hear them.

8

But by the next morning, the prospect of an evening with Lando, alone in the seclusion of Ashleigh House, instead of being a relief in the aftermath of the nuisance calls the evening before, now loomed scarily large. Almost as scary, in fact, as the calls had been.

She dressed for work in her customary white blouse and black skirt. She had a full day, so she'd have plenty to think about and do, effectively distracting her from thoughts — and fears — about the evening ahead of her. But Lizzie's greeting resurrected the anxieties she'd managed to set aside as she drove to work.

'How're the nerves? Don't forget, in the midst of all the excitement this evening, to put our side of the argument against any rent rise.'

'We've already made our feelings on

that subject more than plain, Lizzie. I don't intend to labour the point. It could just make him even more determined. Lando Wheatley didn't strike me as being a man who'd welcome being told what to do.'

'You're not going to say anything?'

'If the opportunity arises, then maybe. But I'm not going to spend the evening banging — '

Lizzie snorted. 'Aren't you now? Maybe that would work better than anything. It's worth a try, at any rate.'

'Banging on about it,' Becca went on, trying to restore some semblance of decency to the conversation. Lizzie could be extremely vulgar at times. She'd embarrassed Becca more than once in other people's company. 'He wants my opinion on his house. Ideas for its renovation, that's all.'

'Hah! 'Course he does. You being such an expert on renovations. Have you even decided what you're going to do in your own cottage yet?'

'Well, no.'

'Exactly,' Lizzie crowed. 'So how do you expect to advise someone else, and on a mansion at that?'

'It's not a mansion, just a large period house.'

'I'd call it a mansion.'

'Anyway, it wasn't my idea.'

'No; I know whose it was. It's just an excuse to get you there. He has some personal intentions towards you, if you ask me.'

'Well, I'm not asking you. Your imagination's working overtime as usual.'

'I think not.' She grinned suggestively.

And that was how the day went on, with Becca trying to disregard her friend's sometimes extremely lewd remarks about the evening ahead. Which meant that she was heartily relieved when the day ended and she could escape and go home. However, she still had what could turn out to be a difficult evening in front of her, and yet again she toyed with the idea of cancelling her visit. She had both of Lando's phone numbers, landline and mobile, but she couldn't bring herself to do that, not so late in the day. It would be rude. Good manners and consideration for others had been something her mother had drilled into her. So much so, that it had become second nature. It still was.

So, unable to come up with an acceptable alternative, she braced herself for whatever the evening might bring, and concentrated on the tricky question of what to wear. She didn't want to bestow the impression of having tried too hard, or even worse, to make him think she was hoping he'd make love to her. In the end, she opted for a just-above-the-knee grey skirt and teamed it with an emerald-green tunic top. A pair of sheer black hold-up stockings gave her legs an attractive sheen.

She studied her reflection in the mirror. Was her neckline a bit low? It did reveal a couple of inches of cleavage. Would he construe that as some sort of invitation? Deciding he might well do, she hastily extracted a chunky necklace from a drawer and put that on. Yes, better, she decided.

She then slipped her arms into a jacket and wound a scarf around her neck. The evenings were unseasonably cold for November. She slid her feet into a pair of four-inch heeled black shoes and checked her wristwatch. It was seven forty. Time to go. She swallowed nervously. After her shame-less behaviour on Wednesday evening, she wouldn't be at all surprised if he wasn't eagerly anticipating making love to her. But maybe his better side would emerge, like it had that evening? She groaned. She had a suspicion that that might be asking too much of the womaniser that Lando was rumoured to be.

★　★　★

The drive to Ashleigh House took less time than Becca had allowed for, so she ended up arriving almost ten minutes early. Several exterior lights came on as she approached, illuminating the area around her, so she had no trouble seeing every part of the building in front of her. She'd never been this close before. She'd only ever glimpsed it from the road, and that was quite a distance away, along a lengthy tree-lined driveway. It was much grander than she'd expected.

Built of cream-coloured brick beneath a steeply sloping grey slate roof, it was two storeys high. She could see a row of dormer windows, although not clearly. They were positioned above the downward beam of the lights. She presumed they were attic rooms; the servants' quarters originally, she guessed. A regiment of chimney pots marched along the rooftop. There was also an impressive number of stone-mullioned windows. She counted thirty in all, and that was just on the front. The main entrance was equally impressive, with a short flight of steps up to a huge oak door that was flanked by a pair of stone pillars and surmounted by a very grand pediment.

She'd done some research on the history of the house and discovered it had originally been built for the Ashleigh family in 1703. They had resided there until the end of the nineteenth century, when the eldest son of that generation, Bertram, had gambled all the wealth away and they'd finally been forced to sell. There'd been many owners since then, none of whom had remained for more than two or three decades, until just months ago when Lando had bought it. Which, as she'd previously concluded, by the relatively young age of thirty-three — or so she'd heard — he'd made enough money to be able to afford a place this grand. Which led her on to the question that had been increasingly troubling her — why on earth was he interested in her, when surely he could have any woman he desired? It couldn't simply be for her ideas on his planned renovation. And why he'd think she'd have any, she couldn't imagine.

She sighed. She couldn't just sit here. She climbed out of the car and slowly ascended the steps to the front door to ring the doorbell.

Why had she agreed to this? For two pins, she'd turn and make a run for it. But it was too late. She heard the sound of footsteps within, and then the door was being pulled open and there stood Lando, smiling down at her.

'Becca, you've come.' His words were laced with muted surprise. Had he expected her to stand him up?

'You did invite me.'

'Yes, but I've been half-expecting a phone call saying you couldn't make it.'

It was her turn to be surprised. She wouldn't have expected that the thought of being stood up would have entered his mind. 'Would you rather I left again?' She made as if to turn around.

'God, no. Please, come in. It's very good to see you.'

Becca stepped inside and found

herself in a hallway that was large enough to contain the entire ground floor of her cottage, as well as a generous portion of the garden. A gracefully curving stairway led up from the black and white chequered floor to a galleried landing. Oil paintings freckled the oak wainscoted walls, and what she assumed were genuine antiques were positioned beneath them. A massive oval table was placed centrally, upon which sat a large shallow bowl of white and bronze chrysanthemums.

'What are you planning to do in here?' she asked. To her, it looked perfect as it was.

'Nothing. I like it as it is. It's the main drawing and dining rooms that need the attention. The kitchen, too, desperately needs updating. I thought I'd concentrate on the ground floor to begin with.'

'How many bedrooms are there?'

'Ten in all. Plus five bathrooms. They all need modernising, but I'm in no hurry. They're all liveable with.'

'It's a rather large house for one person,' she remarked.

'We-ell,' he drawled, 'I hope to fill it with a family sooner rather than later.'

'Oh?' She raised her gaze to meet his. 'I hadn't realised.' She was puzzled. Why was he asking her for suggestions if he had a wife in mind? Surely the wiser course would be to consult the woman who'd be living here. She ignored the faint sensation of dismay that trickled through her at the idea of him getting married.

'Hadn't realised what?' he smoothly asked.

She met his heavy-lidded but glittering gaze. 'Well, that — um, you're preparing to get married.'

'It's not imminent, but I certainly hope to at some point.'

'I would have expected you to be asking whoever it is you plan to — '

'Well, I'm asking you.'

There was that glittering look again. And what the hell did he mean? Not what it sounded like, for sure. Puzzled, she studied him from beneath lowered lids of her own. His build was more powerful than she remembered from their very first meeting all those years ago, and his present air of absolute assurance only increased his sexual appeal. He plainly exercised on a regular basis. Probably had his own gym — well, he certainly had room for it, by the look of this hallway. 'Well, I'm not sure how much I can help you.' She glanced around at the sheer expanse of it all. 'This is well beyond my remit.'

'Why?' He looked genuinely curious about that. 'It's just a house.'

'Yeah. But what a house.'

He grinned at her, reminding her suddenly of the young man she'd first seen. A quiver of desire rippled through her, quickening her breath, making it catch in her throat in an all-too-revealing manner. If he noticed her physical response to him, however, on this occasion he gave no indication of it.

'Come on then. We'll begin in the

kitchen. Ruth, my housekeeper, is in there preparing dinner, but we won't get in her way. There's plenty of room for three of us.'

She'd wondered about staff when it had been him who'd opened the door to her. From the look and size of the house, she'd half-expected a footman in full livery to open it, and had been astonished when it had been Lando himself. She wondered now how many people there were working here. Several, she surmised, to maintain a house like this. Ten bedrooms, five bathrooms — and that was just upstairs. Lord knew how many rooms there were down here.

She followed him out of the hallway and through a door on the far side. She couldn't help it; she gasped when she walked in. 'Room for three of us'? There'd be room in here for a couple of dozen bodies, at least. However big it was, though, it desperately needed modernising. Everything looked very antiquated. The biggest Aga she'd ever seen stood in an alcove that was almost the same size as her own kitchen. There was also a conventional gas range with a six-ring hob. Pans simmered on this, from which arose a delicious aroma. The worktops and cupboards sorely needed replacing; the latter were constructed in a very dark oak, chipped in places and definitely in need of a coat of varnish.

'Ruth,' Lando said to the plump woman who smiled as they walked in, 'meet Becca Seymour. She's here to give me a few ideas.'

Ruth held out a hand to Becca. She could only be thirty-five or thereabouts, Becca guessed. 'How nice to meet you, Becca. Lando's told me about you.'

He has? was Becca's initial thought. *How come? He doesn't actually know all that much.*

'You're in the salon, the Pamper Parlour, I believe?'

'Yes, that's right. I run it with a friend.'

'I've been meaning to pay a visit.'

'Oh, you must come. We'd love to see you. We offer all sorts of services: hair dressing, facials, manicures, pedi.' She stopped talking abruptly. She sounded like an advert. This was borne out by the way Lando was regarding her; his expression was one of subdued mirth. She stared back at him, challenging him to say anything. His grin widened, but all he said was, 'What do you think?'

'Of the kitchen?'

He nodded.

'Well, I think, Ms — ?' She regarded the housekeeper questioningly. She didn't know her surname, and it felt presumptuous to address her by her Christian name.

'Oh, Ruth, please,' the older woman put in. 'We're very informal here.'

'Ruth, then. I think that Ruth is probably the best one to consult about this room. She'd know better than me what's needed.'

Ruth smiled and gave her a surreptitious wink. Becca sensed she'd made a friend. She smiled back.

'Well, I can certainly come up with one or two suggestions,' Ruth instantly volunteered. She'd clearly been waiting for this moment and the chance to voice her own opinion on what was needed. 'The ovens for a start. It would be good to have a new Aga, for instance, and an electric double oven and separate gas hob. A microwave oven would also be a godsend. As for the worktops and cupboards, they need to be lighter. The room's very dark; gloomy, even. It's quite dispiriting at this time of the year, and I have to say, it's not much better in the summer.'

She was right. The gloom had been the first thing to strike Becca. There were four fairly large windows, but the room faced north, so wouldn't get much in the way of sun at any time of the year, as Ruth had pointed out. 'I agree. Maybe white or ivory with granite or marble surfaces? You can get some lovely marbles now. And the floor could also be lightened. Terracotta tiles, maybe, to warm the look of it all.' She glanced down at the floor. 'This slate grey is very cold. You could also incorporate a central island. There's more than enough room. It could act as a breakfast bar as well as storage.' Not that much storage room was needed. The place was vast. There was probably a walk-in pantry somewhere.

Ruth was emphatically nodding. As for Lando, he was looking around, also nodding his approval.

'I think you're right. I'll put your ideas to the kitchen designer, although he's already suggested an island.'

Becca grinned at a beaming Ruth.

'Right then, we'll get out of your way,' Lando said, leading the way back into the hall once more. The drawing and dining rooms were also in fairly good condition, just rather dated. Though taking the period of the house into account, he'd have to be careful about over-egging things. Any updating would need to be done in a sympathetic manner, otherwise he could spoil the look, the entire character of the rooms.

However, Becca felt able to offer a few suggestions.

The drawing room faced south, so would be bright and sunny on a summer's day. The wallpaper was seriously wrong; too patterned, too busy. She suggested something lighter and plainer. 'Maybe a textured finish rather than patterned? Or even a colour wash of some sort? There are some fabulous effects that can be achieved by an experienced decorator.'

The dining room, she went on to suggest, could be lightened too. It was panelled in dark wood from floor to ceiling. The furniture was also dark wood, with burgundy red upholstery. Heavily patterned curtains only added to the lack of light.

'I'd change all of this,' she said. 'Keep the panelling, as it's obviously original, but maybe have lighter wood for the furniture with paler upholstery, to give some contrast? And for the curtains, I'd go for plainer fabric. Maybe pale green, duck-egg blue, a touch of lemon? In watered silk, possibly? The chairs look uncomfortable. Rather than wood, I'd opt for padded and upholstered seats and backs.' There were twelve chairs around a table that would comfortably seat sixteen. She hoped they wouldn't be dining in here. The two of them would be lost in the grandeur of the room.

'In case you're wondering,' Lando suddenly said, 'we'll be eating in the small dining room. It's warmer.' Yet again, he was demonstrating how intuitive he was. 'It's also the room the previous occupants used, so it doesn't need anything doing to it. Well, that's it for the moment, so how about we go into the snug and have a pre-dinner drink? I think you deserve it.' He grinned at her, despatching her pulse into hyperdrive as she anxiously contemplated the rest of the evening alone with him.

9

Becca followed Lando back across the hallway to the door immediately opposite the dining room. They walked into a room that was much more to her liking. For starters, there was a log fire burning in an inglenook fireplace, and to add to the feeling of warmth, it was decorated mainly in shades of burgundy and ivory, and furnished with deep-cushioned settees and armchairs. A flat-screen television, the first she'd seen, was fixed to another wall, and the remaining two walls were lined with fully stacked bookshelves.

'This was originally used as the library,' Lando told her, 'but I decided it was a perfect room for everyday use rather than using the drawing room.'

'It's cosy.' Heavy curtains were drawn across what looked like a fairly large window to one side of the television.

She would have loved to take a look outside, but as it was dark it wouldn't have been much use. So instead she asked, 'How many acres of garden do you have?'

'Twelve. Parcels of land have been gradually sold off over the years. Originally, the estate owned somewhere in the region of several hundred acres. What remains has been professionally landscaped. I doubt I'll do much more to it. You'll have to come in the daytime and have a look round.' He indicated one of the armchairs, the one nearest the fire. She sat down. 'Now, what would you like to drink?'

She opted for her favourite tipple, a glass of red wine. Lando poured himself a gin and tonic. He then positioned himself on the settee, precisely opposite to Becca, where he reclined back against the cushions and took a large mouthful of his drink, all the while subjecting Becca to a heavy-lidded scrutiny.

Becca, running true to form, instantly

began to fidget, tugging at her skirt, which had managed to ride halfway up her thighs, placing her in imminent danger of exposing the lacy tops of her stockings and the inches of bare flesh above.

He gave a small smile, deliberately not looking in that particular direction, before saying, 'You look lovely, Becca. Please stop worrying.'

'I'm not worrying,' she indignantly told him.

'You always fidget then, do you?'

'Not usually.'

'So what's different now?'

She could have said, *The way you're looking at me, as if you'd like to devour me inch by inch*, but she didn't. 'I'm simply making myself comfortable. This settee is very soft. I'm in danger of disappearing down into it.'

'Well if that's all, don't worry. I'll pull you back out.' His smile broadened into a grin, as if he were imagining doing that very thing. 'So, tell me about your salon.'

Relieved to have something more

commonplace to talk about, she did just that. She was briefly tempted to bring up the matter of the rent rise, but decided that might be pushing her luck. Both she and Lizzie had presented their case, so she didn't see any advantage in pursuing it. And as she'd said to Lizzie, such persistent and repetitive arguments against it might simply harden Lando's determination. She didn't have him down as a particularly biddable man; quite the opposite.

The time passed effortlessly, and all of a sudden Ruth was there announcing that dinner was ready. Lando got to his feet and proffered a hand to help Becca up. She thankfully grasped it. She'd been dreading having to indulge in an undignified scramble as she struggled to lift herself from the deep cushion. He then led the way out of the snug, back into the hall and through yet another doorway.

'How many rooms do you have downstairs?'

Ruth answered this. 'Nine, if you

count the laundry, the butler's pantry, and Lando's study.'

'Heavens, and you have to clean them all?'

'Well,' Ruth laughed, 'not just me. I do have help from two local women. They come in on a daily basis.' She proceeded to lead the way into a room that clearly served as a smaller dining room. 'This is also used as a breakfast room. It gets all the morning sun.'

The room was charming and in no need of redecoration. Becca glanced around. There was a set of French doors — the curtains had been left undrawn, although she couldn't see anything of the garden outside — and another fire burned in a small grate. A table, considerably smaller than the one in the main dining room, was laid for two. A vase of lilies sat in the centre, their perfume subtly scenting the room.

Lando pulled out one of the chairs and waited for Becca to sit down before taking his own seat, immediately opposite her once again.

'Okay, as you see, your starters are already on the table, so I'll leave you to it,' Ruth told them.

Becca studied the food set before her. It looked delicious. Cornets of smoked salmon stuffed with huge prawns in a Marie Rose sauce were arranged decoratively on top of a salad of mixed baby leaves and miniature red and yellow tomatoes. Lando lifted a bottle of white wine and raised his eyebrows enquiringly at her. She nodded and he poured some into her glass. She'd have to limit herself; she had to drive home. Though if push came to shove, she could ring for a taxi.

Oh, what the hell. She took a large mouthful. She still hadn't decided what she should do if Lando tried to make love to her. And, judging by the way he was regarding her now, his stare narrowed and intense, that was a very real possibility.

In an attempt to ease the tension that was steadily growing between them, she forked some of the salmon into her mouth and murmured, 'This is delicious.'

'I'm very fortunate to have Ruth.'

'Do you often entertain?' Jeez, what a lame thing to ask. Of course he often entertained. He was a successful businessman, and that was what they did. He probably played a mean game of golf, too.

'Quite a lot. More often than not, it's for business reasons.'

So what did that make her? She certainly couldn't be considered a spot of business. Or maybe she could, if he was counting on persuading her to accept his views on renovating the salon frontage. She glanced around the room, desperate for something to say that sounded halfway intelligent, and came out with, 'Obviously you're very successful, and . . . ' She stopped midsentence. She'd been about to add *must make a lot of money*, but that would sound incredibly crass; tasteless, even.

'And what?'

She cast caution to the wind. 'You've

clearly made a lot of money in a relatively short time.'

He didn't reply. Desperate now to escape the hole she was so industriously digging for herself, Becca impetuously went on, 'By the age of what, thirty-three-ish?'

'Exactly right. Thirty-three. But you've done pretty well yourself, with your own business by the age of . . . what?' He was mocking her, echoing her words back to her. 'Late twenties?'

'Twenty-seven. But don't forget Lizzie and I are partners. The business isn't just mine. I couldn't have done it without her.'

He reclined back into his chair, his fingers toying with the stem of his wine glass. He looked eminently relaxed, unlike her, who felt as tightly drawn as a guitar string. 'I presume the two of you get on well? Partnerships can sometimes prove difficult, if not unworkable, if the relationship isn't a good one.'

'Yes, we do. We've known each other

a long time.' She shrugged. 'Well, if I'm absolutely honest, she can be a bit forthright at times.'

'Yeah.' He grinned. 'I'd got that.'

There was a knock on the door and Ruth entered, carrying a large tray. Lando stood and took it from her, placing it on the nearby sideboard for Ruth to serve from.

The main dish was beef Wellington, served with tiny potatoes, garden peas and miniature carrots. This was eventually followed by a chocolate and raspberry tart and then a selection of cheeses. And throughout it all, the conversation flowed surprisingly smoothly in the wake of the initial awkwardness on Becca's part. They discovered several shared interests: reading — while Becca preferred psychological thrillers, Lando preferred biographies or something historical; a love of good food; music — classical for both of them, with a sideline of classic pop; and politics for Lando, though Becca pulled a face at this, declaring, 'I like it in small doses. I enjoy a well-informed political debate, but that's about it really.' They both enjoyed a good film, but it had to have a strong plotline. 'I can't be doing with all this fantasy stuff,' Becca said. Lando agreed.

And all of a sudden, they'd eaten everything, leading Becca to lean back in her seat and say, 'Wow! I couldn't eat another morsel. That was superb.'

'Glad you enjoyed it. It makes a refreshing change to be with a woman who actually eats and doesn't just shift it round her plate before leaving most of it.'

Becca eyed him. Was that a dig at her? Did he in fact mean she was greedy? Or even worse, fat? He looked back at her. 'I mean that — and no, you're not fat.'

'Right.' As she'd reflected more than once, he seemed to have the ability to detect her thoughts. It was deeply disturbing.

'Come on, then. We'll have our coffee in the snug. I'll put some music on. I'm sure I'll have something to suit us both.'

Becca followed him from the dining room. She hadn't noticed any sort of DVD player in there, so she reckoned it must be very cleverly concealed. A tray of coffee awaited them, and she watched from the armchair she'd rushed to sit in, deciding it would be a safer option than one of the settees. Lando opened a door in a unit disguised as a set of drawers beneath the television screen, and hey presto, there was a DVD player, plus a large collection of discs. He selected one and slid it into the player. The liquid tones of Lionel Ritchie filled the room.

'One of my favourites,' she softly told him.

'That's lucky. It's one of mine too.'

'I thought you were a rock man — Led Zeppelin, Duran Duran, Genesis.'

'Depends on my mood. Right now — ' He looked directly at her. ' — I'm in a romantic frame of mind.' He walked back towards her. There was no mistaking his expression. His look had darkened; his eyes gleamed hotly at her. Never mind dancing, he was intending to make love to her.

Becca's heart leapt. Here it came. The moment she'd known was inevitable. Decision time had arrived.

But when he simply said, 'Dance with me?' she was completely thrown. So much so that when he held out his arms to her, she initially froze. 'Um . . . ' she stammered. He *didn't* want to make love to her. She didn't know what to say. An agonising disappointment engulfed her, which meant that all she could come up with was the pathetic, 'Wh-what about the coffee?'

'Damn the coffee,' he murmured. 'Come here.'

As if in a trance, she got to her feet and walked into his still-open arms. He immediately drew her close, so close she could smell his aftershave, feel his breath feathering her face.

She closed her eyes, helpless to resist the pull of desire. He didn't hesitate.

His grip tightened as he deftly fitted her body against his, ensuring she was acutely aware of every powerful line of him. Her own desire heightened until she could barely breathe. She inhaled sharply as they began to move, slowly, sensuously, in time to the sultry tones of the singer.

Becca made no move to free herself, not even when he lowered his head to hers and buried his face in her hair. Her breathing quickened as her pulse raced madly. Her body felt as if it were on fire. She felt his mouth searching out the softness of her skin, gently sliding down over her face to tenderly caress her arched throat, as his fingers threaded themselves through the strands of her hair, cupping the back of her head. She pushed her head back even further, allowing him the freedom to do as he wished.

She heard his low groan and a thrill of excitement ripped through her. His lips grew more insistent as his hand lowered itself to her hips, where it pressed her even closer. She couldn't mistake his arousal, and her own body responded. She heard him groan again. 'Oh God, Becca,' he said as he moved to her lips, and his mouth captured hers, his tongue moving within and entwine with hers. The hand that had pressed her so close now lifted to enclose a breast, his thumb and forefinger brushing its peak, catapulting her into a frenzy of passion.

It was her turn to groan her desire aloud. They'd stopped dancing by this time; there was no further pretence between them about what it was they wanted. He walked her backwards to the settee and pushed her down onto it. He swiftly followed, positioning her so that she was lying beneath him. His kisses grew in passion, his lovemaking becoming more and more intense.

Becca responded with everything she had. Desire rampaged through her, threatening to engulf her. She'd never felt this way before, not with any man. Her skirt had ridden upwards until it was barely covering her. She watched, mesmerised, as he lowered his head to lavish kisses upon the inches of flesh exposed above her stocking tops. She lifted herself towards him, meeting his lips as they moved, higher . . . Desire savaged her, leaving her gasping in its wake.

Then — what the hell was she doing? What was he doing? His mouth had continued its progression upwards. He was literally ravishing her.

'No,' she gasped. 'Stop -1 don't want . . . '

He instantly froze. She half-raised herself and tried to push him off her, but all he did was lift his head and stare at her, his eyes so dark with passion they were almost black. He remained that way for several seconds before abruptly sitting up, releasing her as he did so.

She began to shiver as she realised what had almost happened. She barely knew him and she'd let him touch her, kiss her intimately. So much so, that if she hadn't halted things, they'd have been making love, fully, totally. Horror engulfed her, brutally replacing the passion she'd felt only seconds before.

'I-I don't want this,' she muttered, frantically pulling her skirt back into place and sitting up.

Lando's breathing was ragged. He continued to stare at her. He seemed beyond speech.

'I don't want this,' she repeated in a low monotone.

'Are you sure about that?' he said. 'Because it sure as hell felt as if you did.'

'Yes, I'm sure.' She spoke low, huskily. 'That's not what I came for, so I-I'd better go. I've done what you asked, made some suggestions for your-your renovations.'

'So you have,' he lazily drawled, for all the world as if nothing at all had happened between them, when in fact it felt as if her whole world had shifted and nothing would ever be the same again. 'However, I think you'd better drink some coffee before you try and drive.'

'I'm fine,' she stiffly told him.

'No, you're not.'

'So if you believe that, why did you try and take advantage of me? What happened to the principles of the other night?' She couldn't believe the cool-ness, the scorn contained within her voice, not when she was shaking so badly inside she felt as if she were being torn apart.

'You'd had a lot more to drink then.'

'In which case, I'm fit to drive now.'

'Becca, please, let me call a taxi for you. I'd drive you back, but I've also had a bit too much for that.'

He was right. Deep down, she knew that.

'Of course, you could stay the night,' he murmured. 'I've got more than enough room.'

Yeah, right, she mused. And who was to say he wouldn't stray into her bedroom? 'No, thanks,' she curtly told him.

'In which case, I'm ringing for a taxi.'

'What about my car?'

'I'll get it delivered back to your cottage first thing in the morning, in case you need it.'

'Okay,' she muttered grudgingly. 'Thanks.'

He regarded her as he lifted his phone and rang a local taxi company. Becca stared back. She could see his frustration. And no wonder. She'd stopped him right in the middle of . . . Why had she done that? she agonised. She'd wanted him every bit as badly as he had her. A lot of men would have been less than gentlemanly about it. But not Lando.

What the hell was wrong with her? Most women would have just enjoyed the moment. Leapt at the chance of being made love to by such a handsome, charismatic man. But that wasn't her way, she admitted. She wanted love, real love that would last, endure; not a fleeting moment or two of passion. And the truth was, she wasn't sure that was what she'd get from Lando.

The taxi arrived within five minutes, to Becca's considerable relief. The silence between them had been embarrassing, and had grown more so with every moment that passed.

'Th-thank you for dinner,' she haltingly said.

'You're welcome,' he stiffly responded.

She was finding it hard to believe that this was the same man who'd been passionately kissing her just a few moments before. He behaved and looked like a stranger — a stranger, moreover, who visibly disliked her; despised her, even.

She went out to the taxicab and climbed in. 'Honeysuckle Cottage,' she told the driver as he moved off. She did cast a backward glance at the house, but Lando had gone.

Lord knew what he must be thinking of her. She closed her eyes; belatedly, her heart aching. He probably had her down as a callous tease — Something

Marco had also accused her of, although in a different context. Maybe they were right, each in their own way; maybe she *was* a tease. Either that, or frightened to commit herself. She should have halted Lando's lovemaking long before she did. In fact, she shouldn't have accepted his invitation to dance in the first place. She'd known she was playing with fire. Well, she'd been well and truly scorched. That would teach her.

Upon returning to the cottage, the first thing she did was put on the kettle. A cup of tea would hopefully put her right, restore her to normal — wouldn't it?

She'd just poured the boiling water into the pot when her landline phone rang. She swallowed nervously. Lando, ringing to apologise? Her heart leapt as she walked into the hall and lifted the receiver. 'Yes?'

There was just silence to start with. But she knew someone was there. She could hear the breathing. 'Who is this?'

Still no answer came, just the continuing sound of heavy breathing. 'Look, whoever this is — ' She didn't manage to finish.

'I know you're seeing other men,' the voice hissed into Becca's ear. 'So I'm warning you — I'll always be there, somewhere nearby, watching, waiting. You're mine, and sooner or later you'll have to admit that and stop wasting both our lives. We can be together. We should be together. Why can't you see that?'

10

Once her heartbeat and emotions had returned to normal, Becca went back into the kitchen. It had to be the same caller as before; the only difference was this time he'd spoken. She frowned. She hadn't recognised the voice. Mind you, why would she have? He'd hissed the words, deliberately, she suspected, so that she wouldn't recognise him. Because it had been a man, that she did know.

Could it have been one of her three dates from the speed-dating evening — Marco, Gary or Andy? It was a reasonable supposition, and out of the three of them, Marco seemed the most likely. He'd been the one who'd exhibited jealousy, possessiveness. Although Andy had sounded as if he'd truly believed they were a perfect match. Could it have been him, in a desperate attempt to convince her he was right? Or was it Marco trying to frighten her into seeing him again? And then there was Gary . . . Any one of them could have looked up her landline number in the phone directory. They each already had her mobile number. In fact, why hadn't whoever it was rung her on that? Once again, she tried the 1471 service and received the same message as before. No number available to return the call. So whoever was responsible was hiding their own number. But then, if their motive was to scare her, they would, wouldn't they?

A chill crept through her as another possibility occurred to her. Lando? For all his coolness, he must have been angry with her, if not furious. Could this be his way of punishing her for rejecting him? Something she was sure he wasn't accustomed to. Yet it didn't feel like something he'd do. Especially not the first silent call. And why would he have done that in any case? She'd agreed to meet him at his house. He'd have had no reason for such a thing. No, Marco was a much better bet. He hadn't liked rejection. Though she hadn't actually ended things between them, he'd done that in a fit of pique. Still, he was the most plausible candidate.

★   ★   ★

The following day was Sunday, and Becca decided to go and visit her grandmother. She hadn't been in over a week, which was unusual for her. She made a point of going at least once a week, twice if she could manage it. Becca knew she looked forward to her arrival, although a lot of the time she'd completely forgotten the previous visit.

Oh — her car. Had Lando returned it as he'd promised? She went to the window that looked out onto the road and saw to her relief that it was there, parked on her driveway. Had he left the key in the ignition? She hurried into the hallway and saw it lying on the doormat. She picked it up, her feelings of guilt about the previous evening resurrecting themselves.

She had to take her share of the blame. She shouldn't have responded to his lovemaking the way she had. He'd been right — she had led him on. Maybe she should ring him and apologise? She reached for her mobile phone, but then, just as she was about to retrieve his number, her nerve failed her. She couldn't do it.

She ate some breakfast and drank several cups of tea before dressing and driving to her gran's care home. It was only a couple of miles away, so it didn't take long, and by eleven o'clock she was ringing the doorbell to be allowed in.

'Hello, Becca,' Samantha, one of the carers, greeted her. 'Your gran will be pleased to see you. She missed you last week.'

'I'm sure she did, but I just couldn't make it. Sorry.' She gave a weak smile.

'Never mind. Her nephew came yesterday afternoon. I didn't actually see him, but — '

Becca stared at the girl. 'Her nephew? Her only nephew is in Canada.'

'Oh.' Samantha looked uncertain; anxious, even. 'Well, that's what he said, apparently.'

'It couldn't have been him. He's never been to England.' She paused. 'What did he look like? How old was he?'

'I'm not sure. I'll check. As I said, I didn't see him. One of the other girls let him in. It was your gran who told me about his visit and who he was.' She peered down at the visitor book, which everyone who visited the home had to sign both on arrival and departure. 'I can't see — oh, hang on. Yesterday — here it is. J. Doe. Three thirty. He left again at four thirty.'

Becca stared at her. 'J. Doe?' John Doe? The name that was given to an unidentified body. It was clearly a false name, and whoever it had been had wanted her to know that. Her heart began to hammer. As unlikely as it seemed, could it be the same man who'd phoned her? But why would he visit her gran? She gnawed at her bottom lip, recalling how she'd told each of her dates about her gran, mainly because they'd quizzed her about her family. She'd even told them the name of the care home that she was in. Oh God. Why had she done that? She frowned. But if it was her anonymous caller, why would he go to the lengths of visiting an old lady? He wouldn't hurt her, would he? Though perhaps he would, as a way of punishing Becca for seeing other men, as he viewed it. But if he didn't tell her who he was, what was the point? They couldn't be together if she had no idea of his identity.

Fear stabbed at her. Maybe she should move her gran. But where to? There weren't that many private homes in this area. At least, not ones that her gran could afford to pay for.

'I'll have a word with Gran. Find out

a bit more.' Although whether her gran would remember enough about the man to give an accurate description was highly debatable. 'Could I have a word with the carer who saw him? Get a description, if possible.' It just might give her a clue to who it might be.

'Yeah, sure. It was Kathryn — oh, there she is. Kathryn, have you got a minute?'

The young woman hurried over. 'Yeah, but it'll have to be just that — a minute. I'm on my way upstairs. Mrs Harding in room sixteen has buzzed.'

Samantha repeated Becca's request, but Kathryn shook her head and said, 'Nothing stood out about him particularly. Um, if I remember rightly, he had dark hair — well, darkish. Quite nice-looking. Sorry, I can't really remember. I only saw him for a couple of minutes, and I see so many visitors.' She shrugged, at the same time giving a rueful smile. 'They all tend to blend into one. Sorry.'

'How old was he?'

Again, she shrugged. 'Not sure. Mid-thirties, I would guess, but it's only a guess.'

Becca sighed. That age and description could fit any one of her suspects for the phone calls. She'd have to rely on her grandmother for more details. But she didn't hold out much hope of that.

Her fears were almost immediately realised. Her grandmother regarded her in confusion. 'My nephew? Oh, dear me. Let me think now. Oh yes, I remember.'

Becca's hopes rose.

'Such a nice man. He said he'd take me out next time, for tea.'

'Yes, Gran, but what did he look like?'

'Look like? Oh, dear, you know me and faces. My eyesight isn't what it used to be.' She grimaced ruefully. 'Is it important, dear?'

'It could be, yes.' Becca hesitated, not wanting to scare her. 'There isn't going to be a next time, I'm afraid. He wasn't your nephew. I don't know who he was.'

Her warning clearly didn't register with her grandmother, because all she went on to say was, 'He brought me some chocolates. Do you want one? They're in my room.'

'No, Gran. I need to know who he was.'

'John something. Yes, that's it. John somebody. Oh dear, I can't remember.' She was beginning to show signs of distress. 'I'm just a stupid old woman. My memory is so bad nowadays. I'm sorry.'

Her heart aching, Becca took her hand. 'It's okay, Gran. It's okay.' But she resolved to see the manageress and instruct her to personally vet anyone other than herself who asked to see her gran.

In fact, when she did manage to see her, Becca asked her to phone and request permission for anyone other than her to visit before allowing them in. She could be here within ten minutes. It should be relatively easy to operate this sort of screening. As far as Becca was aware, she was the only person to visit. Most of her gran's friends had died or were too old themselves to make the trip here. She had no other relatives in the UK. Her sister had emigrated many, many years ago, and had only been back twice in all that time. Which made it extremely improbable that her son would visit his aunt. And he sounded too young anyway. Great-nephew? That could be it. But how had he known where his great-aunt was living? As she understood it, it had been decades since anyone else had communicated with her gran. There wasn't even an address that she could write to, enquiring whether a member of the family had been to the UK.

Becca eventually drove away, her frame of mind one of deep concern. She spent the rest of Sunday catching up on her chores, her mind careering wildly between thoughts of the previous evening's events and anxiety over her grandmother's wellbeing — as well as her own.

She was industriously ironing her clothes ready for work the following day when she heard the sound of a car pulling up outside. As Honeysuckle Cottage was the only house in this part of the lane, it had to be someone to see her. She put the iron down and, with a heart that was hammering with apprehension, went to the window that over looked the road. It was almost nine thirty. Who would be calling at this time?

Gingerly, she peeked around the curtain. It was inky dark by this time, but she should be able to see who it was. She gasped when she saw the silver Jaguar. Lando. What did he want? Although she had a nasty suspicion. But surely he hadn't come simply to continue their argument from the evening before? She was pretty sure he wasn't the person responsible for the phone calls and the visit to her grandmother. So what other reason could he have?

She inched backwards and then to one side. He wouldn't be able to see her now. She could pretend to be out . . . Oh hell no, she couldn't. Her car was parked right outside.

Queen Bee, sensing her anxiety, wound herself around her ankles, meowing loudly. 'Ssh,' she murmured. The doorbell rang. Becca didn't move. Queen Bee meowed again, louder this time. Becca picked her up, cradling her against her chest. 'Ssh.' The bell chimed again, this time for longer. He wasn't going to give up, that was self-evident.

'Ye gods,' she muttered. When it rang a third time, she strode to the door, still holding her pet close to her. She yanked it open and stood, glowering at him. Queen Bee leapt from her arms and ran outside. 'Gee thanks,' she muttered. No support there then? 'What?' she asked very rudely, but frankly she was past caring.

Lando stood and regarded her. 'Do

you make a habit of ignoring your doorbell?'

'Only when it's someone I don't want to see.'

His expression darkened as his eyes narrowed at her. He then asked with pointed and excessive politeness, 'Can I come in? Or do you want to do this on the doorstep?'

Becca leant forwards and glanced up and then down the lane, before saying, 'Why not? There's no one to see — or hear.'

He didn't respond to this, other than to compress his lips into a tight line.

'Oh, come on in then,' she grudgingly invited.

'Thank you,' he murmured. 'It's nice to see you too.'

Becca chose to ignore that piece of sarcasm, even though she acknowledged that she was being extremely rude. It was something she normally tried to avoid at all costs, but there was something about this particular man that seemed to goad her into it. She swung around and led the way into the sitting room before again grudgingly saying, 'Have a seat.'

'Thank you.' He strode to the settee and sat down. He was the picture of composure, relaxing back against the cushions and lifting a leg to rest one ankle on his other knee.

Becca opted for the armchair opposite to him, where she waited silently for him to say what he'd come for.

He didn't speak immediately. In fact, he looked as if he were searching for words; the right words. 'I-I felt I couldn't leave things between us as they ended last night.'

'Why not?'

He looked taken aback at her bluntness. 'We-ell, I feel that some of what happened was my fault, and I want to apologise for — well, rushing you. I usually take things more slowly, but with you . . . '

She waited for him to finish, and when he didn't, she asked, 'With me? What's so different about me?'

He met her gaze with, outwardly at least, composure. Which was more than could be said for her. Her heart rate was practically supersonic and her throat was getting drier by the second.

'Everything.' He spoke huskily, so maybe he wasn't quite as cool as she thought.

'Thanks,' she riposted.

He cocked his head and studied her keenly. 'You must have realised how attracted I am to you.'

Becca said nothing to that. She simply waited.

'And when you responded to me — so readily, so passionately . . . '

She snorted loudly. 'So it's all my fault, the fact that — what was it you said? Oh yes, you rushed me.'

'No,' he quickly replied, 'that's not what I meant. But you did give me the impression that you welcomed my . . . lovemaking.'

'Well, I didn't.'

His gaze sharpened. 'Are you sure about that?'

'Positive.' Could he tell that she was nowhere near as confident of that as her tone suggested?

'Okay. So explain why you responded with such passion?'

'Well, you-you . . . ' she stammered, casting wildly around for a credible reason. 'You took me by surprise.' God, how lame was that? He'd see straight through her.

He didn't disappoint her. 'Oh. He raised an eyebrow. 'Do you always react so heatedly when surprised?' His mouth quivered.

He was actually laughing at her. How dare he? 'No, I don't.'

'Then why did you on that particular occasion?'

'What is this?' she snapped. 'Your version of the Spanish Inquisition?'

'Not at all,' he smoothly said. 'I'm simply trying to understand what happened, exactly, between us.'

'I've just told you. You took me by surprise.'

He continued to study her intently

before his mouth widened in a grin. 'Well, here's a thought. If I warn you that I'm about to kiss you, how will you respond, do you think?'

'I've no idea.' She was quietly confident that he'd do no such thing.

However, when he got to his feet, she knew she was one hundred percent wrong in that assumption. He most certainly would do it. She hurriedly got to her feet as well, and so they stood, a couple of feet apart, staring silently at each other. He inched closer. Becca instantly backed up, only to feel the edge of the armchair pressing against the back of her legs. She could retreat no further. Something flickered in the depths of his eyes as he murmured, 'Shall we try a little experiment?'

Becca's heart was thudding so hard now, she could barely draw breath. He took another step closer, close enough that his breath caressed her face. She shivered.

'I'm going to kiss you.'

'N-no, you're not. If you do, I'll-I'll — '

'You'll what?'

'I'll — '

But before she could think of anything else to say, he'd reached out and pulled her into his arms, taking full possession of her lips. Becca couldn't help herself. Her lips parted beneath his and she found herself clinging to him.

He wrapped his arms even more tightly round her before his hands began caressing her, one lowering to her hips, pulling her close. Once again, she was aware of his physical arousal, and she certainly couldn't mistake her own. A tsunami of passion was swamping her, enflaming her entire body. She lifted her hands to the back of his neck, opening her mouth wider to him. Her breath had caught in her throat, almost suffocating her.

Unexpectedly, he pulled away and stood, staring into her eyes, his own hooded, dark, glittering — and totally unreadable. 'That's interesting. Even when warned, you still respond in the same way. What does that tell you?' he softly asked.

The passion that gleamed at her equalled her own. She shook her head, miles beyond speech. But then, somehow, she gathered her senses together and whispered, 'You tell me, because I haven't a clue.' It was true, she hadn't. She was bewildered, confused. She'd never responded to any man the way she responded to this one.

He smiled, sensuously, seductively, at her. 'I think you want me every bit as much as I want you. So what are we going to do about that?'

She shook her head at him, her eyes wide and luminous.

'Do you know how incredibly beautiful you are?'

Again she shook her head. She seemed to have lost the ability to speak.

'There's a vulnerability about you that makes me want to take care of you.'

'I don't need taking care of,' she

huskily told him. Thank God, she mused, she'd recovered her power of speech. 'I'm a grown woman. I can take care of myself.' But could she? In the wake of the anonymous phone calls and the disturbing visit by a man unknown to herself as well as her grandmother, she was no longer quite as confident of that as she had been.

'I know that. But please, Becca, let me see you again? Let's give this thing between us, whatever it is, a chance.'

'Okay.' She was as shocked by her ready agreement as he manifestly was. He didn't speak, and all Becca could think was that he thought she was beautiful; he wanted her. Yet, there'd been no mention of love. Was this what she wanted? A relationship based on desire, passion? But something within her was urging her to go for it, give it a chance, see what happened. She was lonely. She admitted that. She wanted someone to love. Her life of late consisted of work, and that was all. None of the speed dates had worked out. It was time for something else. And she couldn't deny she was fiercely attracted to Lando; he was right about that.

'Okay,' she repeated. 'Let's give it a go. There's nothing to lose.'

11

Once Lando had left, Becca sat, everything that had just happened replaying in a continuous loop in her head. She'd expected him to make love to her in the wake of her agreement to go on seeing him, but he hadn't made any attempt to do so. He'd even refused her offer of a drink.

'I can't,' he said.

'Why not?'

He'd regarded her, his head to one side, as a small smile played about his lips. 'Guess.'

She'd shaken her head, thoroughly bemused by all that was happening.

'If I stay, we both know what will happen, and I'm not making the same mistake twice.'

'Oh,' was all she felt capable of saying.

'We'll take things slowly. Get to know

each other properly. Will you come out with me on Wednesday evening for a meal? I'll reserve us a table at Grimaldi's.'

Grimaldi's? It was only the most exclusive as well as the most expensive restaurant hereabouts. She'd never been there, but she'd heard about it. She nodded.

'Good. I'll pick you up at seven thirty.'

★ ★ ★

Once he'd gone, she asked herself what had she let herself in for. But more to the point, and distinctly more puzzling, was why someone like Lando Wheatley would be so interested in her. He must have women queuing up — considerably more beautiful women than her — to go out with him. Women from his own world of wealth and glamour.

She still hadn't come up with any sort of answer to that, come the next morning. In fact, her emotions were all over the place. Which must have shown up on her face, because the first thing Lizzie said to her as she walked into the salon was, 'What on earth's up with you? You look as if someone's clobbered you over the head with a sledgehammer.'

'That's the way it feels,' Becca muttered.

'Come on, give. What is it? Who's walloped you? Tell me and I'll go and return the compliment.'

'Lando Wheatley has asked me out on a date.'

Lizzie looked almost as shell-shocked as Becca felt. Her eyes widened and her mouth dropped open. 'What? No way.'

'Yeah.'

Lizzie frowned. 'So can I take it that you went to his house on Saturday to *advise* — ' The word was loaded with sarcasm. ' — him on his house renovations?'

'I did. We had dinner.'

Now it was impatience that Becca

detected in her tone. 'And what happened?'

'That's it. We had dinner.'

Lizzie was eyeing her with unabashed speculation. 'Was that when he asked you out?'

'Uh, no. He-he came to the cottage last evening.'

'Did he now? He's keen, I'll give him that. So are you going?'

Becca nodded. 'On Wednesday. He's taking me to Grimaldi's.'

Lizzie's eyes widened. 'Grimaldi's? You do realise how upmarket that place is, do you?'

'I've heard. Have you ever been?'

Lizzie snorted with mirth. 'God, no. Way out of my league, or anyone else's that I know.'

'I'm not sure what to wear. I was hoping you could give me a clue.'

'Sorry, no can do. Something elegant and classy, I should imagine. You'll be competing with the very rich. Designer dresses and drop-dead shoes every way you turn.'

Becca nibbled at her bottom lip. She didn't really do classy and elegant, mainly because there was nothing in her wardrobe that would fit that description.

'However, on a more optimistic level, you'll be in the perfect position to talk him out of a rent increase.'

Becca didn't respond to that. She'd spotted her first client of the day coming through the door.

For a Monday, things were unusually busy, allowing Becca no time to speak to Lizzie or for Lizzie to speak to her. Which, for once, Becca welcomed. Lizzie could be like a terrier with a tasty bone when she latched on to something she felt strongly about, and she certainly felt strongly about the threatened rent increase. So it was with considerable relief that at the end of the day, Becca called out a hurried goodbye and made her escape.

She drove home quickly, eager to put her feet up with a glass of wine in her hand. She left the car on the driveway, too tired to open up the garage and put it inside. Queen Bee was perched on the kitchen window sill, awaiting her arrival. She had an uncanny instinct for sensing when her mistress was about to arrive. Becca smiled at her pet, even waving, which meant it wasn't until she was mere inches from the door that she spotted the rose.

A single, long-stemmed red rose.

It was lying on the doorstep. In fact, she only just managed to avoid treading on it. She stopped and gazed down upon it for several seconds, before bending over and lifting it up. She sniffed at it. No perfume, disappointingly. She did smile though. Could this be from Lando? She imagined it was the sort of thing he would do.

She glanced around. Was he watching from somewhere close by — to catch her reaction, maybe? Disappointingly, there was no one to be seen. She examined the flower more closely. No sign of wilting, so it couldn't have been there long.

Pulling the key from her handbag, she unlocked the front door and stepped inside, to almost tread on an envelope lying on the doormat. She bent down and picked it up, Queen Bee meowing around her ankles as she did so. 'Okay, I'll pick you up in a minute.'

Printed on the front of the envelope, in large capital letters, was her full name, REBECCA SEYMOUR. That too was the sort of thing Lando might do. He'd said he preferred her full name to Becca.

Smiling once more, she ripped the envelope open and pulled out a single sheet of paper. But her smile instantly turned into a frown as a quiver of uncertainty — of fear, even — pierced her.

She read: 'You know what a red rose means. I love you. I won't give up on you, on us. I know you feel the same deep down, so why are you denying it? Rejecting me so cruelly? I'll warn you again. Don't force me to do something I don't really want to. I'll ring you, so

214

be nice. Be good. Be loving. Be mine.'

This wasn't from Lando. He wouldn't do something like this. She stared again at the rose, which she was still holding, before rereading the words on the sheet of paper.

What the hell did they mean? 'Don't force me to do something I don't want to'? Was the writer of this actually threatening to hurt her if she didn't respond to him? But how was she supposed to do that if she had no idea who he was? It didn't make sense.

She read the words a third time, more slowly, as she struggled to comprehend their meaning. It had to be the man who'd rung her, hissed at her down the phone; the man who'd visited her gran, saying he was her nephew. It couldn't realistically be anyone else. Suddenly, everything became horribly real, threatening, frightening. A sensation of nausea rose from the pit of her stomach.

She had a stalker — some deluded individual who believed she loved him;

believed they had some sort of relationship. She'd read of this sort of thing happening to other women. The stalker could be a complete stranger, someone who intercepted a harmless glance, a polite smile, a murmured word in passing, and believed in his madness that it all indicated love. For him.

She couldn't help thinking that surely no one she knew would do this to her. Even so, Marco came back to mind, and the way he'd stormed off because he believed she'd betrayed him in some way by meeting Gary and Andy. And both of them had seemed keen. Andy, for instance, had thought they were soulmates.

But this sort of thing only happened to celebrities, didn't it? Not an ordinary person like her. Yet, if it was someone she knew . . . Oh, for goodness sake, she was going round and round in circles now.

She regarded the rose again. For all that it was perfect, it now looked menacing. She strode into the kitchen,

Queen Bee following, still meowing, to open the bin and thrust the perfect bloom down inside. The sheet of paper and envelope followed.

She pulled a sachet of cat food from one of the cupboards and squeezed the contents into the cat bowl, which she placed on the floor, murmuring, 'There you are. Enjoy,' before straightening up again and staring through the window to the road beyond. There was no one there. She leant forwards and looked both ways. Still no one.

At that exact moment, the phone rang in the hallway. At first, she didn't move; she felt paralysed, in fact. Then she quickly walked out to it, to stand quite still, staring down at it.

Should she pick it up? Supposing it was the person who was doing all of this to her? Had he been watching her? In which case, he probably knew she was inside the house. She lifted the handset from its base and put it to her ear. 'Yes?' The fear quivered in her voice. Would he hear it and be gratified?

But there was only silence for a few seconds before she heard the sound of someone heavily and deliberately breathing into the mouthpiece.

'Who is this? Answer me.'

A man's voice hoarsely whispered, 'Did you get the rose? My note?'

'Yes,' she snapped. 'Who are you? Why are you doing this?'

'You know why. I love you. I know you feel the same way. Why do you insist on denying it?'

'Who are you?' she cried.

'Think about it and you'll know who I am.' And the line went dead.

Becca slammed the receiver back onto the base before running into the lounge. She slumped down onto the settee to sit, hunched over her knees, her face buried in her hands. She had no idea who was doing this to her. *Think about it*, he'd said, *and you'll know*. But she didn't. It could be anyone. She should ring the police. Although what they'd be able to do, she didn't know.

She hurried back to the kitchen and retrieved the rose, the letter and envelope. She then dialled 999 and told the call handler what was happening to her.

'There'll be someone with you in the next hour,' the woman said.

As it turned out, it was nearer two hours, but at least they came. Two of them, plainclothes detectives. She told them what was happening to her, but as she'd anticipated, there wasn't a lot they could do.

'Has he threatened you physically?' one asked.

'Yes,' she cried. 'Read the note. I'd call that a threat, wouldn't you?'

' We-ell, until he actually does something . . . ' He shrugged.

Evidently there was nothing they could do to stop what was happening. They did take the letter and envelope away with them to check for finger-prints; but as they said, unless the prints were somewhere on their database, that wouldn't help either.

Becca did the only thing she could think of: she opened a bottle of red wine and poured herself a very large glassful, which she proceeded to knock straight back before pouring herself a second. By the time she went to bed, she'd drunk the entire bottleful. Which did ensure she slept deeply the whole night through.

However, that proved a mixed blessing. Because she awoke the following morning, her head pounding, and a sensation of nausea rising steadily within her. Somehow she managed to repress it, even as she asked herself what she had been thinking of, to drink the whole bottle. It was something she almost never did, knowing too well what the end result would be.

Somehow she got herself to work, where Lizzie took one look at her and asked, 'What is it this time? Not Lando Wheatley again?'

'No, a bottle of wine.'

'That's not like you. What's up?'

So Becca told her.

Lizzie was horrified. 'And you've no idea who it was?'

'Not a clue,' Becca mumbled, at the same time as trying to stem another rise of nausea. 'I have wondered whether it's one of my dates from the speed-dating night. Marco, in particular.'

'You don't recognise the voice, then?'

'No; he only ever whispers.' She shivered. 'It gives me the creeps.'

'Have you phoned the police?'

'Yeah, and a fat lot of use they were. He hasn't actually attacked me or hurt me, so . . . ' She shrugged.

'Useless prats,' Lizzie muttered.

'I did think about ringing Marco and asking if it's him.'

'Don't do that. If it is him, it will only encourage him. Try and get him talking next time. He might forget to whisper, giving you the chance to pinpoint exactly who he is.'

'I think he's wise to that tactic. He doesn't stay on the line for long. It doesn't make sense, Lizzie. How can I respond to his demands if I don't know who the hell he is?'

' Sounds like a nutter to me.'

'My thoughts exactly. Which is even more worrying. Who knows what he'll be capable of if I don't do as he wants? I mean, he could be schizophrenic or something. Maybe he hears voices, telling him what to do.'

With the arrival of their first clients, however, they were forced to conclude their conversation. Still, the problem — and the fear — gnawed away at Becca all day. So much so, she was relieved when six o'clock came and she could leave. Though she couldn't say she was particularly looking forward to an evening at home alone. Who knew what her stalker was planning?

'Fancy a drink?' she asked Lizzie.

'Sorry, I can't. I have a date.'

'Oh.' She couldn't hide her dismay at the news.

Lizzie eyed her. 'I could cancel, if you're nervous about going home.'

'No, no. Definitely not. Who's the date with?'

'One of the chaps we met on the speed dating. It's our second date.' She wiggled her eyebrows at Becca. 'He seems keen, so I thought, why not?'

There was nothing else for it but to go home. Becca started to walk to where she'd left the car that morning. It was further than usual. Someone else had nabbed the space she more often than not parked in. As it was already dark, she didn't hang around, but broke into a jog. There weren't many people about, which intensified her nervousness — a nervousness that felt perfectly justified; when, unexpectedly, the back of her neck tingled. She stopped and swivelled her head to look behind her, just as someone — a man, she would have sworn — disappeared around the corner. Could he have been following her?

Without giving herself time to think about the wisdom of what she was doing, she turned and hurried back to the spot where he'd disappeared. She peered along the alleyway that ran adjacent to one of the shops and led to another wider side road. This skirted round the rear of the shops to join the main road leading out of the town.

But she was too late. Whoever it had been had gone, if it had indeed actually been someone and not a figment of her fevered and extremely active imagination. Fear could play strange tricks on the mind. Deciding not to venture any further along the alley — he could be lying in wait? — she turned and hastened back the way she'd come, desperate now to reach the safety of her car. Once inside, she locked all the doors before turning on the ignition and speeding off.

She wasn't even halfway along the lane that led to her cottage when a set of headlights blazed behind her, reflecting back from the interior mirror to practically blind her. She braked as she adjusted the mirror to minimise the glare before she pressed hard again on the accelerator and sped off. The other driver did the same. She positioned her head so she could glance once more into the mirror, squinting against the glare as she did so. But her effort was futile. She couldn't make out either the sort of car it was or who the driver might be. The lane was lined by trees, with enough leaves still clinging to the branches to block most of the light from either the moon or the stars, thus ensuring she could see almost nothing of the car behind her, other than the fact that it was a fairly large vehicle.

Her heartbeat quickened until it was thudding painfully in her chest. He was following her. Fear gripped her then; real fear. She hadn't imagined someone behind her in the town. Though he'd disappeared, he must in fact have retraced his steps along the alleyway and then, unseen by her, followed her back to her car.

The one question that hammered away at her now was what would happen when she reached her cottage and had to stop. She was only a couple of hundred metres away. Should she keep going and hope she could lose him, or brazen it out and confront him?

She decided to leave it until the very last moment to pull onto her driveway and trust that he'd drive straight on. He did, racing by, giving her no chance to identify either the driver or the type of car, other than the fact that, as she'd already detected, it was a large dark-coloured saloon. She sat in her car for several moments, trembling, thoroughly shaken, and praying he wouldn't turn and come back. When nothing happened, she climbed from the driving seat and made a dash for her front door. Fumbling with the keys, she finally managed to get inside and ran directly to the sitting room window.

There were no streetlights this far from town, so it would be well nigh impossible to spot, let alone identify, someone outside. Nonetheless, she stood there for a while, gingerly peering around the edge of the curtain, until she was quite sure there was no one lurking nearby. Only then did she close the curtains and turn on the light.

Her entire body was shaking convulsively. She gave a small sob of despair. This was what he was doing to her. Because it couldn't all be down to her imagination. She conceded it was pretty active at the best of times, but tonight had felt different. The large dark car had definitely been following her, she was positive of that. He'd slowed when she'd slowed, and accelerated when she did.

All of a sudden, she wondered what sort of car Marco drove. Hang on — he'd told her. It was a Jaguar. But what colour and model it was, she had no idea. It could well be a dark shade, and it would most likely be large. She didn't know much about them. And to be honest, most large cars looked the same to her. Jaguars, Mercedes, Volvos, BMWs, Audis . . . they all seemed to come from the same mould, as far as she was concerned. There was one thing that did comfort her — Lando's Jaguar was silver, so he definitely hadn't been her stalker.

Tears stung her eyes as she resisted the temptation to open a bottle of wine, instead filling the kettle and switching it on. *Get a grip*, she told herself. *What can he do to you, when all's said and done?* Sadly, she didn't have an answer to that, or at least not one that didn't terrify her.

12

She only managed to calm down by repeatedly telling herself that her stalker, whoever he was, was simply trying to intimidate her; bully her, even. He wouldn't actually harm her, would he? After all, he wanted her to love him, be with him. How would harming her achieve that? It wouldn't.

And come the next morning, she'd almost convinced herself of that — until she walked out to her car and found an envelope pushed beneath her wind-screen wiper. Once again, her name was printed on the front. With a feeling of dread, she opened it and pulled out the single sheet of paper. She read: 'Did you enjoy our drive together last evening? I saw you, staring at me in your mirror. We'll do it again — soon. I love you and I know you love me. Admit it. You'll have to in the end. PS.

Have you worked out who I am yet?'

So it hadn't been some random driver going the same way as her, as she'd fleetingly hoped; he had been actively pursuing her. Which meant he must either have been watching her, or he already knew all about her. He knew where she worked and what time she left in the evening. He knew where she lived. If it were a stranger doing this, would he be asking if she'd worked out who he was? It either had to be someone she knew, or he was so delusional, so deranged, that he really did believe they were enjoying some sort of relationship, and she was simply playing hard to get. He believed, in his insanity, that she did in fact know who he was.

A penetrating chill encompassed her. Supposing this madness, if that was what it was, resulted in him actually trying to harm her? Yet despite her disturbing reflections, doubt still lingered. Her stranger theory felt unrealistic; improbable. So much so, she struggled to convince herself it had to be someone she knew. That way, it somehow felt less terrifying.

She drove to work, glancing repeatedly into her driving mirror, terrified at the prospect of sighting a car, any car, behind her. But there wasn't one, at least not until she reached the high street; then of course there were several. None, however, resembled the vehicle of the previous evening. She managed to park right outside the salon, which was a massive relief, as she wouldn't have to walk back to her car later. And she'd have a very effective form of distraction this evening. She was meeting Lando. He was the one she could be sure of. He'd have no reason to stalk and threaten her; she'd agreed to date him.

Still, her sense of impending danger grew. If her stalker was watching her, as his calls and letters implied he was, how would he view her going out with another man — right under his nose, so to speak? Would that be what ultimately drove him to violence?

Lizzie showed deep concern when she spotted her friend's ashen face. 'Is he still bothering you?'

Becca nodded and pulled the envelope from her coat pocket. 'This was on my car.'

Lizzie read it. 'What drive?'

'He followed me home last evening after work. He obviously views that as a drive together.'

'Flippin' hell, this is getting serious, if not dangerous.'

'Tell me about it.'

Lizzie eyed her more than a little apprehensively. 'I hope you don't mind, but last night I told Sam what was happening. He rang me just as I was going out. He's as worried about you as I am.'

'Oh?'

'Yeah. He said you can always call him if you're really frightened. His new place is only ten minutes away. He'll come round. Mind you, the mobile's no good there, so you'd need to call him on the landline.' She gave Becca the new number.

'Well, that's kind, but — '

'It's okay, no strings attached. I can assure you it's not some kind of ploy to get back with you; he told me he's seeing someone at the moment. Again, I haven't met her.' She rolled her eyes. 'He seems to have a phobia about introducing girlfriends to me. But he can't stop talking about her. Jane something or other. They're discussing her moving in with him, anyway; that's how serious it is.'

'Jane?' Becca was surprised. 'It wasn't that long ago I saw him with someone called Mel. So, what was it? Love at first sight or something?'

'I know. It's all a bit too quick for my liking.' Lizzie pulled a face this time. 'But I'm glad he's met someone at long last that he cares about. And his new house is plenty big enough for two. I went to visit just after he moved in. I was very impressed. The garden alone is almost an acre. He's had some sort of workshop erected, which he's intending to use for his photographic work.'

Sam was a good photographer. He'd won prizes. He'd even talked about starting up a studio of some sort at one time. Clearly he was about to do just that.

'Still keen then, is he?'

'Oh Lord, yes. And this woman is some sort of model, I believe. So he's been putting together a portfolio for her.'

'Well, good for him, and thank him for me for his offer. I might well take him up on it.'

Becca had been relieved as well as happy to know that Sam had finally found someone he could make a life with. She'd felt so bad at the time about ending things with him. He'd been distraught, pleading with her not to do it; to give him another chance. The fact that he'd seemed unable to move on to other relationships had only deepened her guilt. But the news that he'd finally met someone, someone he actually wanted to spend his life with, cheered her immensely.

Not that she had time to ponder the matter; she was virtually booked solid for the day. She hoped she wouldn't be too weary to enjoy her evening with Lando. Lando . . . Her heart lurched several times as she thought about him. She still found it hard to believe that a man like him — gorgeous, rich, sexy as hell — could be interested in her. Interested enough to the point of being willing to wait for her; give her time. She smiled to herself. She had a sneaking suspicion it wouldn't take long.

Her first client, who was having a manicure, smiled at her as she took her seat. 'It must be a man,' she murmured. 'Only a man could inspire that dewy-eyed look.'

'It is. A very special man.'

And he was, she finally admitted. Very special indeed, and she wasn't going to let him slip through her fingers. Okay, maybe it wouldn't last forever, but she was going to enjoy every second for as long as it did.

By the time seven o'clock came round, however, that brave resolve felt distinctly shaky. She was way out of his league, and way out of her comfort zone.

She eyed herself in the mirror in her bedroom. Was she dressy enough? He'd surely be accustomed to escorting women attired in the very latest fashion; cost-a-bomb designer wear, in all probability. What was he going to think of her dress? There was no way it could be mistaken for designer wear. But it was the one she'd worn for her first date with Marco, and he'd liked it. It was quite plain, with a fitted bodice and a fairly low-cut neckline that revealed a couple of inches of cleavage; the skirt gently flared to finish just above her knees. Despite its simplicity, the green silky fabric made the most of her hair and eyes.

She was still considering it, her head tilted to one side, trying to view it through Lando's eyes, when she heard the sound of a car drawing up outside. She darted to the window and looked out. It was him. Well, it was too late now for second thoughts, either about the date or what she was wearing. She had to go through with it.

She slipped on a jacket and picked up her handbag, belatedly feeling as if it was the guillotine awaiting her rather than a handsome man. However, by the time she opened the door, she'd calmed her flutter of nerves and had even mustered a smile.

His gaze raked her and his polite smile widened into an appreciative grin. 'You look ravishing,' he murmured throatily. 'Beautiful, in fact.'

'Thank you.' Miraculously, her voice was steady. But then her nervousness flooded back, and to her horror she heard herself saying, 'So do you.' Oh, good grief, what the hell had made her say that? How ridiculous she must sound.

That was swiftly confirmed for her.

Amusement gleamed in the slate-coloured eyes, the tiny gold flecks that she'd glimpsed once before illuminating them so that they were almost silver. 'Well, I've never been told I'm beautiful before. Thank you — I think.' He gave a throaty chuckle.

Becca felt her face warming. 'S-sorry, I didn't mean . . . ' She gnawed at her lower lip, furious with herself for her unutterable stupidity; naivety even. Who, in their right mind described a man as beautiful? No wonder he was laughing at her.

'I know you didn't.' His eyes darkened and narrowed at her — the look that she was becoming familiar with and which invariably sent her pulse haywire. 'I'm just teasing you. Don't look so worried.'

'I'm not,' she protested, trying to muster some semblance of dignity. She stepped out of the house and pulled the door closed behind her. Queen Bee was in her usual position, on the kitchen windowsill, looking out. She waved a hand to her pet, only to immediately think Lando would believe she was loopy as well as naive, waving to a cat.

He rested a hand in the middle of her back and steered her towards the car, then settled her inside before striding round to the driver's side and taking his own seat. Once there, he swivelled to look directly at her.

'There's no need to look so scared. We're just two people going out for a meal together.'

'I know that,' she said. 'I'm not scared.' But even she could detect the quiver of misgiving in her voice, so Lando surely would.

This suspicion was confirmed when he murmured, 'Really? I'm not going to try to eat you.'

'I know that too.' Her tone was a sharp one. Even so, she asked herself, did she know that? She recalled the way he'd kissed her the other evening. It had been hungry; demanding.

'Becca, I've said we'll take things slowly. I meant that — truly.'

She stared at him, her green eyes wide and luminous. She watched as he took a deep breath. *Hmm*, she mused, *not quite so composed as he's making out, then.* For some strange reason, that made her feel better; less isolated in her nervousness.

'We'll go at your pace.' He lowered his voice and muttered, 'I'll certainly try.'

Becca glared at him. She suspected she hadn't been meant to hear that. 'Look, if you can't . . . ' She was fully prepared to get out of the car and return to the house. Because the truth was, not only did she not trust him to keep his word, but she didn't trust herself not to respond if he did begin to make love to her.

'I can. I promise. You have nothing to worry about.' He looked away from her then and turned the ignition key.

Becca continued to regard him. There was a brooding look to him, underpinned by a somewhat grim half-smile.

The engine purred into life and the car pulled away from the kerbside. Neither of them noticed the lone figure standing in the shadow of a large tree a little further along the lane, watching intently as they left.

★ ★ ★

It took a mere ten minutes to reach Grimaldi's, and neither of them had spoken the whole way. The tension within the car was such that Becca found herself wishing she hadn't agreed to come. She wondered belatedly if Lando shared that sentiment. She wouldn't be surprised. He couldn't be used to escorting such an unworldly woman; one seemingly unable to make any sort of conversation, even the most mundane. She felt wretched.

But if Lando did feel that way, he gave no sign of it. He expertly parked the car in what looked to Becca a very small space indeed in front of the restaurant, before he climbed out and strode round to open her door for her. He was courteous but cool. They went inside to be greeted warmly by a smiling maître d'.

'Good evening, Mr Wheatley. How are you? So nice to see you again.'

'Good evening, Ricardo.'

The man smiled as he turned to Becca. 'May I take your coat, madam?'

'Thank you.' Becca took it off and handed it to him.

'Now,' he went on, 'a drink in the bar first, or would you like to go straight to your table? It's your usual one, Mr Wheatley.'

'We'll go to the table, Ricardo. Thank you.'

He indicated that Becca go first, with Ricardo leading the way. Their table was shielded from the view of the other diners by a large potted palm. It provided absolute and total privacy. Becca wasn't sure how she felt about that. She was a people-watcher, loving to fabricate her own stories about them, imagining their life histories. But apart from that, it would have been helpful to be able to watch others if the conversation between her and Lando should flag.

'We'll have a bottle of my usual champagne,' Lando told Ricardo.

Ricardo inclined his head, murmuring, 'Certainly.' He then handed them a menu each, which another waiter had given to him.

Once they were seated, Becca asked, in an attempt to start the conversation between them and end a silence that had grown increasingly uncomfortable, 'Do you come here often, then?' Oh, good Lord, of course he did. The head waiter knew him by name, for heaven's sake. The only difference between those other occasions and this one would be the woman he brought with him. Doubtless, the others had considerably more sophistication than her. And they wouldn't ask stupidly juvenile questions.

However, if Lando shared the same reflection, again he didn't show it. 'Now and then,' he told her. 'It's mainly business clients. It's not always convenient to entertain at home.'

No, it wouldn't be. Ruth must have a day off at least each week, maybe more, and she couldn't see Lando cooking for guests. He'd be far too accustomed to having everything done for him.

A waiter brought the champagne and popped the cork before pouring the foaming liquid into glass flutes. Lando lifted his and said, 'To us. To a long and fruitful . . . ' He paused. Becca held her breath, waiting for whatever was coming next. ' . . . relationship.' His gaze gleamed at her over the rim of his glass as he took a mouthful.

Relationship? Was that what they were embarking upon? Deciding to amend that description — it was, after all, early days yet — she said, 'To friendship.'

Heavy lids instantly shielded whatever thoughts he might be entertaining about that correction. As for Becca, she took a large gulp of the frothy liquid and promptly hiccupped. She was then forced to watch as Lando tried very hard to suppress his grin.

'Please, try to stop worrying,' was all he said, however.

How did he do that — pinpoint her thoughts so accurately? She glowered at him. It didn't make a scrap of difference.

'I meant what I said. We'll take things at your pace. Now, what would you like to eat?'

They made their choices; and after they'd given their orders to the waiter, Lando said, 'Tell me about yourself and your family?'

'I've told you all there is to know.' She shrugged. 'Tell me about yours instead.'

'We-ell, my parents live just outside of Worcester. I have a brother, Andrew. He lives in the same area. He's married to Stella, and they have two daughters, Ellie and Claire, five and three respectively.'

'Do you see much of them?'

'Not as much as I'd like. Mainly because I travel quite extensively on business, so it's not that easy.'

'Do they come and see you? Maybe they could offer some advice on your restorations?'

'Oh, no. They're all into contemporary homes. They think I'm mad to buy something so ancient. They do come and visit though. We'll spend Christmas together.' He regarded her reflectively before asking, 'What will you be doing for Christmas?'

'Don't know yet. I'll probably spend a lot of time with Gran, but she gets worried and anxious if I take her out of the care home, so I tend to go there instead.'

'Maybe you could join us at mine — when you're not at the home, that is?'

That took her completely by surprise. So much so, she had no answer to it.

'Becca?'

'Um — well, I think that might be rushing things a little; be a bit premature. I mean, what would your family think?'

'I've no idea, but I'm sure they'd make you very welcome. They're always telling me it's time I committed myself.'

She stared at him now, completely lost for words. What the hell did that mean? That he was committed to her?

'Too soon?'

She nodded, totally dumbstruck.

'Okay, fine. Anyway, here's our food. But if you change your mind about Christmas, let me know.'

The conversation after that took a more casual direction, much to Becca's relief. She simply didn't know what to make of his offer and his subsequent remarks.

Once they'd finished their meal, Ricardo brought their coats, handing Becca's jacket to Lando. He helped her into it, his fingers brushing her cheek at one point, despatching her senses into complete turmoil. She was forced to fight the urge to nuzzle her cheek against his fingers. She couldn't help noticing the half-smile Lando gave, though. He'd done it again — sensed her physical response to him. Which meant the next question was, would he take advantage of her weakness once they were alone? She suspected he would, and she was astonished by the flood of longing that swamped her.

The roads were almost empty on the way home, which ensured it only took moments to reach her cottage. Again, they didn't speak, not until he was parking the car at the end of her driveway. Then he turned to her, his eyes glittering at her through the darkness.

Becca heard herself whispering, 'Would you like to come in?'

He didn't need words; his expression spoke for him. Becca opened her own door this time and climbed out. Lando followed suit. They quickly headed for the cottage.

Once again, they didn't notice the figure, who stiffened before swinging away to melt into the darkness of the night, muttering angrily, 'Will you never learn? You keep on defying me. Denying our love. Clearly I'm going to have to punish you, force you to notice me. To love me. To forget every other man. And, fortunately, I have the means to do that.'

13

Becca unlocked the front door, her body aching with a deep longing. Once they were both inside, she pushed it shut and stood, her hands down behind her and her back pressed to the door, as she quietly asked, 'Would you like a coffee?'

Lando gave her a lingering look before saying, 'No. I'm sorry, Becca — I know I promised, but . . . ' He gave a low groan. ' . . . I just want you. Tell me to go, right now, if that's what you'd rather do.'

She didn't answer. She simply reached for him, muttering, 'No, I don't want you to go.' She lifted her face up to his, whispering, 'I-I want you too.'

She didn't have to utter another word. He wrapped his arms around her as he bent his head and proceeded to ravish her mouth. Becca clung to him, every part of her aflame with desire. His thigh slid between hers as his hands began to move, caressing, cupping, touching her so tenderly, Becca surrendered completely to him.

And then he was pulling away, his eyes blazing with passion as he stared down at her. 'Not here,' he muttered hoarsely.

She led him into the sitting room and straight to the settee. They fell onto it as one, where Lando wasted no time pulling her close again.

'Oh God,' he moaned, 'if you don't want this, you'd better stop me now, because — '

'Ssh, I do,' she told him. 'I do.'

That was all he needed to hear. He bent over her, pulling her beneath him, as she returned his kisses with everything that was in her. She'd never before felt passion like this. A need so great, she was powerless to deny it.

He reached around her and unzipped her dress, tugging it downwards to reveal her lacy bra and the tops of her full breasts. He kissed the bare flesh. 'God, you're so beautiful,' he groaned. 'I want you so much.'

'Me too,' Becca muttered.

He raised his head and regarded her, his eyes tender and dark. 'Are you sure about this?'

'Yes, yes,' she insisted. 'Please — don't stop.'

So he didn't. He made love to her, passionately, ardently, yet with heart-aching tenderness, until finally he made her his, totally. For the first time in her life, Becca felt complete, whole.

Lando propped himself up on one elbow and, gazing down at her, murmured, 'I love you, Becca; really love you.' For a second, then, he looked unsure. 'Is that a bit premature?'

Becca smiled at him tenderly, lovingly. 'No. I love you too, and I'd love it if you called me Rebecca from now on. It seems right, somehow.' She smiled shakily up at him. 'Special.'

'You're special. So very special. Rebecca.' He breathed the word, making it sound so right. Suddenly, Becca sounded so ordinary; wrong, in fact. Juvenile. It was time everyone called her by her full name, even Lizzie.

She looked up at him from beneath provocatively lowered lashes. 'Shall we go upstairs? My bed is considerably more comfortable than this old settee.'

'This old settee,' he firmly began, 'will always have a special place in my heart. It's the place we first made love. But yes, I'd love to go upstairs.' His grin then was nothing short of wolfish. 'And do it all over again.'

* * *

Rebecca awoke the next morning to the sight of the sun slanting through the curtains. It felt like a good omen. She sighed contentedly and turned to look at the man at her side. He was still asleep, breathing slowly and softly. It gave her the opportunity to gaze her fill; to absorb everything about him — every line, every crease of his handsome face. She still couldn't quite believe it. Lando Wheatley loved her; really loved her. She hugged herself rapturously and then realised he was grinning broadly, even though his eyes were still closed.

'You're awake,' she accusingly said.

His eyes snapped open as he made a grab for her. 'I most certainly am, and desperately hungry — for you, for more of what we did last night.' And there was that wolfish grin again.

She laughed out loud, snuggling up to his chest. 'Well, you can't have it. I have to get to the salon. Lizzie will wonder where I am if I don't get going right away.'

'Oh.' He looked genuinely crestfallen.

She giggled and dropped a kiss upon his parted lips. He immediately held her closer. 'Are you absolutely sure?' he huskily asked. 'I can't tempt you?'

''Fraid not.' But the kiss quickly took on a life of its own until she had to drag herself free and leap from the bed. 'Bags the shower first,' she laughed as she started to run from the room. 'Oh, there's just one thing.'

'What's that, then?'

'The planned rent rise.' She widened her eyes alluringly at him, and made a big play of fluttering her lashes at him.

'Consider it cancelled,' he groaned.

'For everyone?'

'Yes.' He gave an even deeper groan.

She skipped back to the bed and kissed him deeply, lovingly, sensuously, before once again dragging herself from his arms and carrying on to the bathroom.

'Little minx,' she heard him mutter from behind her.

★   ★   ★

Lizzie took one look at her radiant face and sighed. 'So you've capitulated? Good night, was it?'

'Oh, Lizzie, wonderful. You have no idea.'

'Oh, I think I have. You're literally glowing.'

'He's wonderful; truly wonderful.'

Lizzie raised both eyebrows. 'Good. That should help in any campaign against a rent rise.'

'You can stop worrying about it. It's not happening.'

'Wow.' Lizzie was eyeing her with a great deal of interest now. 'How did you manage that?'

'Oh, I have my ways.' She gave a small, satisfied smile.

'I'm sure you do.' Lizzie eyed her knowingly. 'When are you moving in?'

'Moving in?'

'Yeah, with Mr Wonderful. I presume that's the next step?'

'Good Lord, not yet. We haven't even discussed that. It's early days.'

'I s'pose. Are you seeing him again tonight?'

'No. Sadly, he's off on business. He'll be gone all day and not back till late.' She gave a wicked smile. 'Anyway, I need my rest. It was a busy night.' This was followed by another even saucier grin.

'You haven't even asked how my date went.'

'Sorry. How did your date go?'

'Rubbish. Looks like I'm single once again.'

★ ★ ★

Rebecca felt as if she was walking on air all day. By the time she returned to the cottage, however, she was exhausted. She smiled to herself. And she knew exactly why. A hectic night of the most glorious lovemaking. She'd have a bath, she decided, and an early night. Another smile lifted the corners of her mouth as she thought, who knew what tomorrow night would bring?

She prepared herself a snack and watched a bit of TV as she ate it. She then went into the kitchen to tidy things away, glancing through the window as she rinsed her plate.

An owl hooted from a nearby tree. Not a scary sound this time, but a friendly one. She peered out of the window, her face pressed close to the glass. She'd love to catch a glimpse —

She froze.

There was someone out there, standing motionless on the opposite side of the lane to her cottage. It looked like a man who was wearing some sort of long coat with a hood pulled well down over his face. It was difficult to see much more detail than that.

What on earth was he doing? She jerked back. Could this be the man who'd been stalking her? It must be. She couldn't think of any other reason for someone to be out there in the dark, just staring at the cottage. Had he seen her looking out? Oh God, it had to be him. But why was he suddenly growing bolder? What had precipitated that? Her pulse quickened. Would he approach the house?

She should call the police. Maybe they'd catch him this time. Or . . . she recalled Sam's offer. He could get here much faster than the police would. Genuinely frightened now, she hurried into the sitting room, to where she'd left her handbag. She'd written Sam's new landline number in her address book. She hadn't got round to entering it into her mobile phone directory. It was no good ringing his mobile, because as Lizzie had told her, there was no signal. Once she found it, she dialled it. But the phone rang out several times before she heard his voice announcing that he wasn't in at present but to please leave a message. She did, her voice breathy and panicked. She then returned to the kitchen window and looked out. Whoever had been there had disappeared. Where to? To watch from another vantage point? Or was he somewhere in the shadows, trying to gain access to her home?

She watched for several moments, but he didn't reappear. After half an hour, she decided to ring Sam and tell him not to bother coming to the cottage. The panic was over. The mystery man had gone.

Once more, she was forced to leave a

message. But this time, Sam rang back within a couple of minutes.

'Bex, are you okay? I've only just got your messages. I was out in my workshop. No extension phone out there, sadly. It's something I'm going to have to sort out. Do you want me to come round? I know the stalker's gone, but I could check things out for you.'

'No, it's fine.' But she couldn't prevent her voice from trembling. 'I'm fine.'

'No, you're not. I tell you what — come here instead. You can spend the evening. Hell, stay the night. I'll fetch you.'

'No, really. It's too much bother.'

'No, it isn't. I insist. You can meet Jane. You'll like her.'

'Oh, is she there?'

'Yeah.'

'Well, okay.' She had to admit, now that her stalker had actually shown himself right outside of her cottage, she was genuinely scared as she asked herself what he might do next. And the truth was, she'd feel a hundred times better about going to Sam's if his girlfriend was there. Though she did wonder fleetingly why she hadn't picked up the phone when it rang. Maybe she'd been outside with Sam? Yes, that must be it.

She did momentarily consider ringing Lando, but she was loath to do that. He'd have to come all the way back from Manchester, although she supposed he could already be on his way. Even so, it could be some time before he actually got here. And she hadn't told him what was happening, in any case. An omission she'd remedy when she saw him the following day.

She waited by the kitchen window, so she saw the exact moment that a black car pulled up outside. A quiver of fear ran through her. She didn't recognise the vehicle, or the person inside — mainly because the passenger door was facing the house, so she didn't have a clear view of the driver. But it must be Sam — mustn't it? It couldn't be the person who was stalking her. Why would he have been initially standing outside, and then go to the trouble of returning in a car? But when she'd been dating Sam, he'd driven a gunmetal-grey VW Golf, and Lizzie hadn't mentioned that he'd changed it.

Gingerly, she went to open the front door, prepared to slam it shut again if it was anyone else out there. So she was hugely relieved to see that it was Sam. He was a few metres away, walking along the lane, closely inspecting the hedgerows on either side before turning and doing the same thing in the opposite direction. Rebecca felt immensely and instantly reassured. He really did care.

He swung and saw her standing in the doorway. 'No sign of anyone. I won't come in. Are you ready to leave?'

'Yes.' She stepped outside and closed the door behind her. She'd left plenty of food and water for Queen Bee, and there was a cat flap in the back door, so she could get out if she needed to.

She saw Sam glance at her handbag. 'Is that all you're bringing? You should stay the night.'

'I've got my toothbrush and some clean underwear just in case.' She patted the side of the bag. 'Are you sure this is okay? Jane won't mind?'

'Her father just rang. Her mother's sick, so she's gone there. She said to apologise.'

'Oh.' Rebecca felt a stab of uncertainty then.

Her expression must have reflected that, because Sam went on with a reassuring smile, 'No worries. Hopefully she'll return later. She hasn't actually moved in yet, but she stays overnight quite often.'

'And if she doesn't come back, won't she mind me staying in her absence?'

'Of course not,' he scoffed. 'I've told her all about you and what old friends we are. She's very keen to meet you, as a matter of fact. So come on, climb in and we'll get going. You haven't seen my new place.' He sounded like a small boy, excited over a new toy. He'd always been the same over any new possession. Rebecca smiled to herself.

'You've also got a new car, I see.'

'Yeah. Top-of-the-range BMW. I've only had it a couple of weeks.'

'Like it?'

'Oh yes.'

'And the house — happy there?'

'I sure am. It's what I've always wanted. A proper home of my own. Complete with the requisite wife and two children, naturally.' He slanted a smile at her. 'I'm working on that.'

'I'm glad you're happy, Sam — really I am.'

'So how about you? Anyone special?'

'We-ell, there could be, but it's early days yet.' She was deliberately vague. She didn't want to jinx things by appearing too confident. She'd done that a few times before, and then within a couple of weeks it had all started to go wrong. She was determined that wouldn't happen this time.

Thankfully, Sam didn't push her,

other than to give her a darting sideways glance. She didn't respond, so he started up the engine and pulled onto her driveway to turn the car around. He didn't speak as he performed the manoeuvre and then headed towards his own house. She assumed he was concentrating on his driving. When the silence continued, though, she glanced again at him. He was staring fixedly through the windscreen. He'd never been a very talkative man, but even so, he was being unusually silent even for Sam. Rebecca again felt a stab of unease.

'Sam — ?'

He swivelled his head and looked at her. 'So who is he, then? This someone in your life?'

'I'd rather not say.'

'Oh, go on. I won't tell anyone, promise.' His gaze narrowed at her, intense, questioning.

'No, I'd really rather not, if you don't mind.'

He rolled his eyes and shrugged, as if

her refusal to say anything was of no consequence. 'You women and your little secrets. You're all the same, making a big deal of everything.'

She didn't respond to this sarcasm. In fact, she was beginning to wish she hadn't taken him up on his offer. However, she had, so she'd just have to get on with things. Sam had always resented her having secrets. He'd wanted to know her every thought, every interest. There'd been times, quite a few of them as she recalled, when she'd felt almost suffocated. Clearly he hadn't changed. Maybe she'd get a taxi home again after an hour or so. He wouldn't like it, but tough.

It didn't take long to reach his house. It was a substantial double-fronted red-brick building, she saw, one of only two detached houses. They were situated well apart, so he and Jane would have their privacy. Rebecca had driven past a couple of times but had never taken much notice. They were fairly ordinary-looking houses, after all.

'Is it Victorian?'

'Yes. I prefer older houses. More character, don't you think?' He seemed to have got over his displeasure with her refusal to name her special man, so she felt herself relaxing once more. 'There's a good-sized garden out back. It takes a bit of work keeping it in order, but do you know, I enjoy it. Makes a break from staring through a camera lens.'

'Does Jane help?'

He glanced at her enquiringly.

'With the garden?'

'Oh, not likely. Might break a fingernail,' he scoffed.

Which seemed an odd comment from a man supposedly so deeply in love. She glanced at him as he parked on the driveway, once again experiencing that pricking of unease. Why oh why hadn't she brought her own car? She could have left when she wanted then. Now she'd either have to depend on Sam running her home, if that's what she decided to do, or call a taxi. He wasn't going to like that. He could have a bit of a temper, she recalled, when things didn't go his way.

'Welcome to my humble home.'

Humble? That wasn't the word she would have used to describe it. He must be doing well, better than he'd been when they'd been dating, if he could afford a house like this. She could see what looked like a double garage, and next to that a gate leading, she presumed, to the garden at the rear of the house. She spotted the tops of several trees running in a straight line beyond that, supposedly along the perimeter of the garden. They were surprisingly large trees; birch, she thought, and maybe beech. Clearly to accommodate such trees, the garden was a spacious one.

'Nice,' she remarked.

'Come on then, out you get. I'll show you around. The guest bedroom's always kept made up, so there's no problem there. And you must see my workshop. It's the thing I'm most proud of.'

'Lizzie told me about it. I must say I'm curious.'

He opened the front door and ushered her inside. She found herself in a square entrance hallway with a couple of doors leading off it, one on each side.

'Dining room,' he pointed at one. Then at the other, saying, 'Through-lounge.' Stairs rose up out of the hall before it narrowed into a short passageway. He led her along it. 'There's a cloakroom.' He pointed at yet another door. 'And this here is the kitchen.' They walked into a large fully fitted space. 'There's a small laundry through there.' He pointed to yet another door.

'This room's nice,' she said. 'I'm planning something similar for mine, although it's nowhere near as big as this.'

'Made a start, have you?' he asked as he strode towards what was obviously a back door. He turned the key to open it.

'No, not yet. I just haven't had the time, what with work and . . . '

'Dating?' He raised an eyebrow at her.

Rebecca chose not to respond to that. Whether she dated or not was nothing to do with him.

In the face of her silence, he went on, 'Still, you've found someone now — even if you refuse to name him.'

Her smile was a cool one. It had been a mistake to take him up on his offer. She should have known he'd be like this, Jane or no Jane — despite Lizzie's reassurances. Sam was never going to change. She'd make her escape as soon as good manners permitted.

'Okay. So, time to see my workshop.'

'Won't it be too dark for that?'

'No; I've had an electric cable laid to it. I need it for evening work.' He gave an abrupt laugh. 'I've even been known to stay all night.'

'Well, that is commitment. Okay, lead

on then.' She hitched her bag more securely onto her shoulder and followed him out into the night.

They trod across a broad stretch of perfectly cut damp grass. The lawn, she could see, was edged by flower beds, at the back of which grew the trees she'd already spotted from the driveway. 'I bet this looks great in the summer,' she told him.

'It does, but I want to do a lot more to it. Ah, here we are. My pride and joy.' He unlocked the heavy padlock and then stood to one side to allow her inside.

Her initial impression as she took a couple of steps in was of two walls completely covered in photographs and a long workbench along another. Her next was of a wooden chair and what looked like an inflatable mattress lying on the floor. A duvet had been flung over it. There was a lidded bucket in the corner, as well as a chest of drawers upon which sat a shallow basin with a large jug and a towel by the side of it.

So he wasn't joking; he really did spend nights out here. She wondered what Jane thought about that. She turned to ask him, but before she could utter as much as a word, he'd taken a step back and slammed the door in her face. She heard the sound of a key turning in the padlock on the other side, and then Sam's voice.

'If I can't have you, no one else can — not even your special someone.' He bit out the final two words. 'So you have a good, long think about that, and I'll be back in the morning to hear what you have to say.'

14

Rebecca was too stunned initially to react. What on earth was he playing at?

'Sam, Sam!' she shouted, thumping on the door with clenched fists. 'What the hell are you doing, locking me in? This isn't funny. You can't just — '

'Oh, but I can,' he said.

She stopped banging and instead stared at the door. Was he playing some sort of joke? She pressed her ear against it. She could hear him outside, breathing. Something stirred inside her then. She knew that sound. It sounded like — oh God. It had been Sam all along. He was her stalker. No wonder she'd thought she recognised the BMW. It had been the vehicle behind her in the lane. But why would he have done such a thing — deliberately set out to scare her; terrify her?

She put her hand to her forehead,

trying to calm her turbulent thoughts. To try and make sense of it. Why would he do something like this? He had Jane now. Why did he still want her — so much that he'd gone to the lengths of locking her in? Oh dear God. What was she to do? Keep him talking, convince him of the stupidity of what he was doing? Convince him to let her out? But above all, she needed to stay calm; to come up with the best course of action.

'Wh-what about Jane? What will she say when she knows what you've done?'

He gave a snort of laughter. 'You're so gullible, Bex, but then you always were. You and Lizzie. There is no Jane. Never has been. But I knew if I told Lizzie there was someone, she'd tell you, and maybe you'd be jealous enough to come back to me. But no, you're still seeing another man. How could you?' There was silence then, before he went on, 'There's never been anyone but you for me. You know that. Yet you've thrown everything back in my face. Flaunting all those men in front of me.'

She almost said, *There've only been four, and two of those were just one date,* but decided that might just inflame the situation even more. So she contented herself with saying, 'They've meant nothing. They were just for fun.'

'You say that now, but what about that Italian-looking chap? Yes, I actually saw you coming out of the White Hart with him. You looked very keen on him. Lovey-dovey, as I recall.'

'No, no. It's over. He wasn't my type.'

But it was as if she hadn't spoken. 'It's true the next one you weren't so happy with. You told me as much.' His tone hardened. 'And so, finally, we come to Wheatley. He's the someone special, isn't he? You didn't have to tell me. I guessed straight away. I saw the way you were together in the pub, all gooey-eyed. You even let him kiss you one night out in the street. Oh yes, I saw you. You didn't see me. And what happened when he drove you home after the pub? After I offered to drive you? Did you go to bed with him?'

'No,' she cried. 'We're just friends.'

'I don't believe you.'

'It's true. Please, Sam — let me out.'

'No, not until you agree to come back to me. We're meant to be together. I keep telling you that, but you just won't listen, will you? We were a perfect match, you and I. But you just threw it all away. Well, things are set to change. I'm making sure of that.'

There was evidently no point in attempting to make him see reason. Instead, she decided to voice her suspicions. 'You're the one who's been stalking me. The one who's been phoning, sending me anonymous letters, following me in your car. You left the rose.'

But if she'd been hoping to shame him into freeing her, she couldn't have been more wrong. 'Clever girl,' he snorted with cynical-sounding laughter. 'You got there finally. It took you long enough. I thought you'd guess it was me straight away.'

'Why would I?' she quietly asked. 'You never signed your name.'

But it was as if she hadn't spoken. 'I tried so hard to tell you that you and I belong together, but you just wouldn't listen, would you? All this could have been avoided. I've been so patient, waiting.'

'So was it you who visited my gran?'

'Yeah. Bet that really worried you, didn't it? Great name, wasn't it? John Doe.' And he gave another snort of laughter.

'Sam, you really shouldn't be doing this. It's not funny; it's crazy. What will Lizzie say?'

'Lizzie? She won't say anything. She agrees with me and thinks we should be together.'

'No, she doesn't. She knows that's not going to happen. Please, let me out. We'll say no more about this then.'

'Sorry, but I can't do that, not until you see sense.'

'You can't do this.' Her voice rose as panic began to take over. 'You can't keep me here.'

'Oh, but I can. No one will know. The neighbours are far enough away not to hear anything. In any case, they're out all day, both of them. I've soundproofed the walls. The only window is triple-glazed.'

She glanced upwards at the skylight. She couldn't possibly reach it, not even by standing on the chair. He must have prepared all of this especially for her. The notion chilled her. She began to shiver as she belatedly realised she had no idea what he would be capable of. He'd clearly lost his mind, was totally irrational. She had to keep him talking. Somehow make him see sense. See the criminality of what he was doing; what the consequences could be.

She folded her arms across her chest and took a deep breath. Screaming angry words wouldn't achieve anything, not in his present state of mind. All it would do would be to harden his determination to keep her locked up until she gave in to him.

'How long have you been planning this, Sam?'

'Not long. Only since you started seeing other men. I knew then it was time to take action. To force you to see sense. To see that I'm the man for you and always have been. It's lucky I bought this house. Must have known I'd have need of it someday. It's perfect: secluded, has a big garden. Neighbours a good distance away. You can scream and shout all you want. As I said, no one will hear you. So get a good night's sleep, and we'll talk again in the morning. Hopefully you'll be in a better frame of mind. More open to reason.'

Rebecca's mind worked frantically then. 'Lizzie will wonder where I am tomorrow when I don't turn up to the salon. I'm never late. She'll ring me.'

But there was no answer. He'd gone. She really lost it then. 'Sam, Sam,' she screamed. 'Goddammit, let me out. You can't do this.' She kicked at the door, hard. 'Ouch,' she groaned as her toes bent painfully backwards. 'Lizzie will miss me,' she added in a whisper.

But it was no good. He was no longer out there.

She swung and looked around; really looked. Her eyes widened in shocked disbelief as she took in what she hadn't noticed before. Photos of her, some blown up, others the normal size, covered two walls, all taken at different times obviously, and completely unnoticed by her. She moved closer, the feeling of horror growing inside. There she was walking round town, going into the salon, inside the salon, working, captured through the window, somehow — with a telephoto lens, she guessed. Outside her house, climbing into her car, climbing out of her car. He'd been stalking her, photographing her, for weeks, and she hadn't noticed a damned thing. All to create this record of everything she did, every day. What did he do? Stand here, as she was doing, gazing his fill?

She covered her mouth with her hand as she groaned. This . . . this was the work of a man completely obsessed — obsessed with her; dangerously obsessed. She looked around once more. It hadn't all been lies. She could see what she guessed were items he needed for his photography, so he really did work out here.

But none of that looked as if it would help her to escape. Once again, she asked herself that all-important question. What would he do if she didn't agree to stay with him? Would he hurt her? Was he capable of something like that? The possibilities chilled her, made her shiver even more. Violently, in fact.

She began to look for a way of escape. But it was in vain. He'd taken every precaution against that. There wasn't a window other than the skylight, and that had a blind pulled down over it. She had no hope of heaving something up at it and smashing the glass as a way of attracting someone's attention; any-one's. And, as she'd already concluded, it was way too high for her to reach, even standing on the chair.

She slumped down onto the chair, still clutching her bag to her. Her phone. She unzipped the bag and pulled it out. There could be a chance — but she gave a sob of despair. Just as Lizzie had told her, there was no signal. What the hell was she to do? She recalled his words, 'If I can't have you, no one can.'

As the sheer hopelessness of her situation dawned, she covered her face with both hands and began to weep — noisily; desperately. Tears spilled over, tears that seeped through her fingers to run down the back of her hands and over her wrists.

It must have been him outside the cottage this evening. He'd known she'd most likely phone him. As he'd admitted, that was why he'd said what he'd said to Lizzie. Why he'd told her about his make-believe girlfriend, Jane.

To make the two of them believe he was over Rebecca, to make her feel safe coming here with him. And all the time he'd been planning to imprison her. To force her to do what he wanted. It was undoubtedly the thinking of a crazed individual. Someone who'd lost all sense of what was right and what was wrong.

What should she do? Lie to him? Tell him she'd stay with him? But then what? The minute she tried to run, he'd certainly stop her. But he couldn't keep her here indefinitely — could he? Memories of news stories she'd heard about women kept imprisoned by men for years hammered at her. He could.

But people would start to search for her within a day or two. She'd be found — wouldn't she? Eventually? That could take a while, though. Nobody, not even Lizzie, would suspect Sam. This was down to her. She had to help herself; no one else was going to do it. She had to use her ingenuity. Come up with a plan for escape.

For starters, she'd make a fingertip search of the workshop, make sure there really wasn't a way out. She tore photographs off the walls, casting them onto the floor, revealing bare-board walls to her gaze and fingertips. She swiftly discovered there was no way out. The walls were impenetrable; double thickness, she guessed, and probably lined with soundproofing material if Sam was to be believed. She took a closer look at the items on the bench, but there was nothing she could use as a tool to try and force the door open. She stood in the centre of the wooden floor and regarded the bucket in the corner. It was clearly intended for use as a toilet. She went over to it and lifted the lid. He'd even provided a toilet roll. She studied the jug next. It was full of water. He'd thought of everything. And as hateful as the idea was, she needed to use the bucket. When she was done, she added some of the water from the jug to it, trying to reduce the stench before fixing the lid back on.

Revolting — but then the seed of an idea implanted itself in her brain. Come morning, she'd probably have used it at least a couple of times, maybe more. If she then added all the water from the jug to the contents, she'd have a sizable amount of liquid.

Supposing she hurled it over him, aimed it at his head the minute he entered? It would blind him for several seconds, giving her the time she needed to make a run for it.

But would it work? It had to. It was the only plan she had.

Feeling fractionally better, she lay down on the mattress and pulled the duvet over her. She then added her jacket. The night was growing cold. She shivered, as much from fear as anything. She was never going to be able to sleep.

But, astonishingly, she did eventually. Not for long stretches of time, mainly because she was forced to get up and use the bucket twice more. Still, it meant the level of liquid was growing.

With added water, it should be more than enough to blind him temporarily, affording her the opportunity to escape. She just prayed the side gate wouldn't be locked — that would be the quickest way out. Less chance of him recovering and stopping her than if she went through the house.

When she finally awoke fully, she felt refreshed and galvanised by the prospect of escape. She struggled to her feet, used the bucket once more, and then added the rest of the water in the jug. Just over half a bucketful. More than enough.

She placed it a couple of feet in front of the door, where she could grab it the second she heard Sam sliding the key into the padlock. She then slipped her jacket back on and slid her shoulder bag over her head so that it fitted securely across her body, but wouldn't inhibit her escape. And then she waited.

It was nearing ten thirty, and she was starting to wonder if he was intending to leave her all day when she heard the sounds of his approach. He'd clearly been intent on punishing her by leaving her this long with just her own thoughts and fears for company. Either that, or he'd hoped if he left her alone long enough she'd have reached the conclusion that he wanted. That she'd agree to stay with him.

Her stomach was clenching with apprehension as well as hunger. It had been hours since she'd last eaten. It sounded as if he was carrying a tray by the sounds of china rattling. Which meant his hands would be full, allowing her more time to make her escape.

She removed the lid from the bucket, picked it up, and waited, tense and shaking with nerves. If this didn't work, he was going to be so angry. God knew what he'd do then.

She listened as he fumbled with the padlock. It took him a couple of minutes, so she guessed he'd put the tray down to unlock the door and then picked it up again. The door swung open and he strode in. He was totally unprepared for what happened next.

She lifted the bucket chest high and heaved the contents straight at his head. He didn't see it coming. The tray crashed to the floor as he shouted, 'What the hell — ?' The liquid swamped his head and shoulders. He coughed and spluttered; he was totally blinded — exactly as she'd planned. She threw the bucket to one side and ran straight at him. She pushed him hard and he fell backwards to the ground. She rushed past him and out of the still open door.

'Hey,' he roared. 'You bitch — I'll get you for this.'

But he was still floundering about on the floor, trying to shake the water off and rub his eyes clear.

As for Rebecca, she ran for her life, heading up the garden, straight for the gate. She grabbed the handle and twisted it. And glory be, it opened. She sped through, along the drive and into the lane. She turned left, the way Sam had brought her and the direction that would lead her back to town, and ran as fast as she could, fear lending wings to her feet and legs.

She'd been running for what felt like several minutes before she heard the sound of a car coming up behind her. She slowed, peering over her shoulder, terrified it would be Sam, giving chase in his car.

But it wasn't. It was a woman. Rebecca flagged her down, praying she wouldn't drive straight past. She didn't. She stopped, opened the passenger window, and asked, 'Are you okay? Do you want a lift somewhere?'

It seemed only a matter of minutes before the driver, Jenny, was dropping her in front of the salon. She spotted Lando's Jaguar immediately — Lizzie must have rung him — and then the police car.

'Looks like your partner's already phoned the police.'

She'd told Jenny what had happened to her. She'd been horrified, and had wanted to take her straight to the nearest police station. But Rebecca had said, 'No, my business partner will be very worried by now. I want to see her first.' Clearly she'd been right.

She hurried inside to discover Lizzie pacing the floor, her face ashen with anxiety. Lando was standing to one side, his face the colour of skimmed milk also, and distorted with lines of worry as he spoke to one of two plainclothes policemen. One was holding a notepad in his hand, and writing down whatever it was Lando was saying.

Lizzie was the first to spot her. She shrieked, 'Where have you been? I've been ringing and ringing you. Your mobile, your landline, nothing. I eventually rang Lando, thinking you might be with him. When he told me you weren't, I started to really worry. So I told him about the stalker.'

Lando had moved to her side by this time. His tone was a tense one as he asked, 'Why didn't you tell me that yourself?'

She smiled weakly up at him, her eyes shining with tears. 'I-I'm sorry. I was planning to. Bu-but I was beaten to it.'

'What do you mean? What's happened?' Belatedly sensing her deep distress, he slipped an arm about her waist, pulling her to his side.

Unable to speak for a moment, she simply shook her head.

'Tell me.' He was frowning down at her. 'What's happened?'

So she did, in a voice that shook and trembled. What Sam had done, the photos he'd spent hours taking, what he'd wanted of her, and then finally how she'd managed to escape.

At first as Lando listened to her, he couldn't seem to speak. His face had whitened and his eyes darkened until he looked almost ready to explode. 'My God,' he said through tightly clenched lips. 'You should have told me what was happening.'

'What could you have done?' she quietly asked.

'For starters, I'd have employed a bodyguard for you.'

Rebecca stared speechlessly at him. As for Lizzie, for once she'd been rendered entirely mute as she struggled to take in all that her friend was saying.

Lando went on, still clearly in a state of shock, 'He could have seriously hurt you.'

'I don't think he would have done that.' But she'd had the very same thought herself, hadn't she?

Lando seemed to gather himself together then and went on, 'After Lizzie rang me, I went to your cottage. Your car was still there, but you clearly weren't. I had a really good look around, hammered on the door, called through the letterbox, peered through windows; you were nowhere to be seen. It was at that point that I became really worried and realised something was seriously wrong. I'd rung you last evening but got no reply, so I'd assumed you were out somewhere and had maybe turned off your mobile. And when you still didn't answer your phone this morning, I just assumed you were busy. Then, when Lizzie rang me and I went to the cottage but still couldn't find you, we phoned the police. God, I'm so sorry. I should have realised sooner something was wrong.'

'But why would you have — ?' Rebecca murmured. 'I should have told you what was happening.'

By this time, Lizzie was in tears of shock and utter disbelief. 'I can't believe Sam did that,' she cried. 'I don't understand. Why would he?'

'To force me to go back to him. He intended keeping me there until I agreed.'

'But wasn't Jane there?'

'There is no Jane. He made her up.'

'He made her up? Why would he do something like that? What was the point?'

'To fool us both into believing he was with someone else, happily with her, and over me. He knew if he told you, you'd tell me, so naturally I'd have no worries about going with him when he offered to take me to his house. He came to the cottage last evening and stood outside in the dark, disguised in a hooded coat, to frighten me and make me ring him. And it worked,' she bitterly told them. 'I expected Jane to be there, and when she wasn't, he told me she'd been called away. And I went with him, fool that I was. I should have known there was something not quite right about it.'

Lizzie regarded her apprehensively then. 'You're not going to press charges, are you?'

'Yes. I'm sorry, Lizzie, but I can't risk him trying something else, as he might do if he's allowed to get away with it.'

Lando interrupted at this point, his expression almost as anguished as hers must be. 'Did he hurt you?' He had both arms around her by this time and was gazing searchingly into her eyes. She knew what he was thinking. Had Sam raped her?

Rebecca shook her head. 'No; not

physically, anyway. Mentally there might be a scar or two, but I'm sure I'll get over it.'

One of the detectives, who'd been listening to all of this intently, as well as making notes on his pad, interrupted to say, 'Okay, so we need a full statement from you detailing everything that's happened.'

When she'd done as he asked, she turned to Lizzie. 'I'm sorry, Lizzie, but I can't let it go. He has to be stopped.'

'I know, I know. I'm just sorry I didn't realise the state of mind he was in. He fooled me too. I'm so sorry, Becca, for what he's put you through.'

Lando again cut in. 'Right. I'm taking you home to the cottage first — to pack a few things — and then we're going to my place, where you'll stay until Sam's taken into custody. You won't be safe on your own. He's clearly deeply disturbed, as well as delusional, so who knows what he'll do next.'

Rebecca didn't argue with him. He

was right. She wouldn't feel safe alone in her cottage.

Lando then gave the detectives his home address and phone number, saying, 'You can contact us there. We want to know the minute you've got him.'

But things didn't work out like that.

That evening, the detective who'd done most of the questioning phoned and asked to speak to Rebecca.

'I'm sorry, Ms Seymour, but Mr Hutton has disappeared. We searched the house and garden, but he's not there. Don't worry, though; we'll find him. We've circulated full descriptions of him and his car to all air and sea ports. We have his license number, so he won't get far.'

'What now?' she cried to Lando.

'You stay here — with me.'

'But my cottage . . .'

'Sell it. Move in with me. It'll be easier to plan our wedding.'

She blinked at him. 'Wedding? Did I miss something here?'

'I'm sorry.' He grimaced nervously. It was the first time she'd glimpsed such an emotion in him, and it made her love him even more than she did already. 'Will you marry me? I love you so much. I'll go down on one knee if that's what it takes.'

She laughed. 'That won't be necessary.'

'So — ?' He pulled her into his arms. 'Will you?'

'Mmm.' She pretended to give the matter some serious consideration while casting a provocative glance up at him.

'Rebecca,' he warned.

She gave a throaty laugh. 'Of course I will. I love you too.'

He pulled her close and tilted her head up towards him, then bent down to kiss her, but stopped an inch from her lips. His eyes narrowed, tantalisingly, teasingly.

Rebecca gave a grunt of impatience, and lifting a hand to the back of his neck, pulled him to her.

'Impatient minx,' he muttered, right

before claiming her mouth and kissing her long and hard. Then he lifted her into his arms and carried her upstairs.

The following day, the same detective who'd rung to say Sam had disappeared rang again with better news. 'We've caught Mr Hutton. He's safely in police custody.'

And suddenly, the future seemed a gloriously secure and rapturous one to Rebecca. She was with the man she loved, the man who loved her — and, what was more, she had a wedding to plan. She really and truly couldn't think of anything more perfect.